THE CORRUPTION OF

HAROLD HOSKINS

A NOVEL

By John Malone

CHARTERHOUSE · New York

THE CORRUPTION OF HAROLD HOSKINS

COPYRIGHT © 1973 BY JOHN MALONE

Chapter 7 appeared in a somewhat different
form under the title "Ground Glass" in
New American Review, No. 3, April 1968.

LIBRARY OF CONGRESS CATALOG CARD NUMBER: 72-92638

MANUFACTURED IN THE UNITED STATES OF AMERICA

For my parents
with love and gratitude

THE CORRUPTION OF

HAROLD HOSKINS

1/Cleanth

DEAN HOPPER did not look up from his desk until Harold had crossed the length of the room. "Ah, yes," he said, "Hello, Harold."

"Hello, sir," said Harold.

"I have a letter here from your mother, Harold. You are aware of its contents, I expect."

"I'm not sure, sir."

"Really? I find that odd. Your mother is getting married, it seems."

"Yes, sir," said Harold. "Oddly enough."

"I beg your pardon?"

"Nothing, sir."

"She has asked that you be allowed to attend the wedding, this weekend. Surely you are aware of the fact?"

"I'm not surprised, sir."

The dean wrinkled his brow. "It is a closed weekend, of course. I could have wished your mother had perused the calendar, Harold, what with mid-term exams coming up next week."

"Yes, sir," said Harold. "I'm sure she'll understand why I can't come."

"No such explanations will be necessary, Harold. Your

grades are excellent—and it is not after all every day that a boy's mother gets married." The dean smiled expansively for a second or two.

"At this school, sir?"

"I don't follow you, Harold."

"Nothing, sir."

"Come now, Harold, out with it. If you have something to say, you should say it. I won't have this pussyfooting around. It's unmanly, Harold."

"Yes, sir. I mean at Broken-Home Prep, sir?"

"I am not interested in impertinence, Harold. I shall have to give you a demerit for that remark."

."I apologize for coming out with it, sir," said Harold.

"Whom is your mother marrying, Harold?" asked the dean as he filled out the demerit card with his gold pen.

"His name is Samuel Lazer, sir. He's an artist, I guess."

"Not the junk sculptor, Harold?"

"Yes, sir."

"I admire his work, Harold. So vital, so contemporary."

"He's a creep, sir."

"I don't believe I heard that remark, Harold. Cynicism will get you nowhere in this world. Why is it that you dislike him, if I may ask?" The dean began tapping his pen against the blotter.

"I've only met him once, sir, so it's a little hard to say exactly. Mutual distrust, I guess."

"Well, Harold, that is surely a barrier that can be expected to fall with the passage of time."

"I doubt it, sir."

"Do I take it that you don't want to go to this wedding, Harold?"

"Yes, sir."

"The unity of the family is a most important matter, Harold. I think in fact that it would be safe to say that it is the cornerstone of morality."

"That's building on sand, wouldn't you say, sir?"

"That will be quite enough, Harold."

"I apologize, sir."

"Nevertheless, I find your attitude disturbing."

"I agree with you, sir. My attitude is very disturbed."

The dean regarded him silently for a moment, tapping his pen faster and faster. "Cleverness, Harold, can be carried to excess, even in a grown man, and in one as young as yourself it is entirely misplaced."

"Oh, I agree with you, sir. I often feel entirely misplaced."

"A clean mind in a clean body is what we strive for here, Harold."

"I just took a shower, sir," said Harold. "That's where Mr. Sidebottom found me, in fact. To give me the message that you wanted to see me, I mean. He said he'd looked everywhere for me."

"Are you trying to tell me something, Harold?"

"What about, sir?"

"About Mr. Sidebottom, Harold."

"I'm sure I couldn't tell you anything about Mr. Sidebottom you don't already know, sir, even though he does strive to become close with his boys."

"Mr. Sidebottom is a very dedicated teacher and housemaster, Harold. So long as a man's actions are within bounds, we cannot pass judgment upon his unexpressed desires. That is one of the cornerstones of a free society. I am sure that you are old enough to understand what I mean."

"Certainly, sir," said Harold. "Mr. Sidebottom said just last week, in reference to the building of the British Empire, I think it was, that the cornerstone of civilization is hypocrisy, sir."

"That will be all, Harold," said the dean, handing him his sign-out slip. "You may leave after your last class tomorrow."

"Thank you, sir," said Harold. "I'm very grateful for this opportunity to strengthen the unity of my family."

*   *   *

"Harold, darling," said his mother as he stepped off the train. "You look so pale. Are you working too hard?"

"Too much sex," said the Creep. "Those boarding schools are jungles of perversion."

"You'll embarrass the boy," said his mother, linking arms with her son.

"I wish you wouldn't embarrass me like that," said Harold.

"I'm so glad they let you out, darling. It wouldn't have been the same without you."

"Is Dad coming?" asked Harold.

"Your father wasn't invited," said his mother, unlinking her arm from his.

"It won't be the same without him," said Harold.

"Darling, don't be unkind. You aren't bitter, are you? I should so hate for you to be bitter."

"Of course the kid's bitter," said the Creep. "To him you're a symbol, a big M, not a person."

"Oh, Harold," said his mother, her voice swooping in dismay, "you must understand. I am your mother, of course, but it is also true I am a person."

"Yes, Mother, I know."

"I have hopes and fears like you," said his mother. "And passions. Darling, I have passions, you know."

"Prick her and she will bleed," said the Creep.

"Yes, Mother, I know," said Harold.

She dazzled him with a smile. Well, anyway, she smiled. "I knew you'd understand, my love. You're a man now, of course. You were sure to understand. I knew it in my heart."

Harold sighed and opened the door of the Ferrari at the curb.

"How much did it cost?" he asked.

"That's a secret, darling," said his mother. "I gave it to Sam as a wedding present."

"Oh," said Harold. He was silent for a moment. "Can I have one when I graduate next year?" he asked.

"One what, my love?"

"Ferrari," said Harold.

"Of course, if that's what you want," said his mother.

"Thank you," said Harold. "It's nice to know that you care."

*   *   *

"Call me Sam," said the Creep, when he had Harold alone.

"Sam," said Harold.

"Would you like a cigarette?" asked Sam.

"You're trying to make friends with me," said Harold.

"Don't be so frank, kid, it doesn't help things at all."

"Okay, Sam."

Sam eyed him narrowly. "I'll try again," he said. "Would you like a cigarette?"

"Sure," said Harold, taking one from the blue pack of Gitanes. "Thanks a lot."

"I suppose you've started drinking, too."

"Drinking?" said Harold.

"Like your mother," said Sam.

Harold sighed. "I was trying not to be frank," he said.

"You're just trying to bug me, that's all."

"You're right, I'm just trying to bug you," said Harold.

"Don't be so frank," said Sam, offering a light.

"I can tell this is a foreign cigarette," said Harold. "It tastes like dried dandelions."

"Look, kid, I came from a broken home myself. Don't think you can get away with this act with me."

"Wouldn't you know," said Harold.

"What's wrong with you kids, anyway?" said Sam. "You're so goddam complacent, the lot of you."

"We're emulating Ike," said Harold. "Wind us up and we do nothing at all."

"Screw Eisenhower," said Sam. "Besides, he did his thing in the war. You gotta challenge life, kid." He gestured with his big hands, the fingernails encrusted with paint.

"Life's a filthy mess," said Harold. "I like things to be neat. I'm for cleanth."

"You're for what?"

"Cleanth," said Harold, this time with certainty. "It's an extension of a philosophy they advocate at school."

"At school?"

"Well, sort of," said Harold.

*   *   *

"Who are you?" asked Harold. Among the plethora of faces, new and old, he had scouted her out on the sun porch. He took her to be a sign of hope.

"I'm here for the wedding," she said, shaking her long blond hair, blond, very blond.

"I figured that," said Harold.

"You must be Harold," she said.

"You must be a friend of my mother's," said Harold.

"No," said the girl, shaking her head, rippling her hair.

"An ex-mistress of Sam's," suggested Harold.

The girl raised an eyebrow. "Hardly."

"Well, you never know around here. My mother likes bohemian living."

"So I gathered," said the girl.

"Do I have to keep guessing?" asked Harold.

"Certainly," said the girl. "It keeps me amused."

"If I guess right, can I ball you?" asked Harold.

"Don't be rude," said the girl. Her eyes were as green as her dress.

"I'm learning to be callous," said Harold. "It's a form of self-defense."

"You don't need any defenses with me," said the girl. "I'm on your side."

"Which side is that?" asked Harold.

"I'm for cleanth," said the girl.

"You've been talking to Sam."

"What's Sam got to do with it?"

"I told him about cleanth. I just made it up."

"No, I haven't been talking to Sam. I just know, that's all."

"We must be made for each other," said Harold.

"I suppose it's possible," said the girl.

"I'd really like to ball you," said Harold.

"I'll consider it—if you can guess who I am."

Harold sighed. "Do you want to know the truth?"

"Of course."

"Life is hard enough without you," said Harold.

* * *

"You must be Harold," said the young man, closing in fast in the rose garden.

"Harold who?" said Harold.

"I've seen your picture," said the young man. "It's all over the house."

"I'm here for the wedding," said Harold.

"Naturally. Your mother is so fond of you. She's always talking about you."

"God help me," said Harold.

"I've been dying to meet you. Shall we sit here on this bench?"

"I'm taking a walk," said Harold.

"Oh, that's fine, I don't mind walking."

"Naturally," said Harold.

"You're better looking than your pictures even, you know," said the young man, advocating the virtues of comradeship.

"Oh, I know," said Harold. "I have cleanth. It shows up better in person."

"It's a quality of prep-school boys," said the young man.

"What is?"

"Cleanth."

"How does everyone know so much about cleanth? I only made it up today."

"You aren't necessarily the first, you know."

"No, I'm usually the last," said Harold.

"You're more sophisticated than I thought you'd be," said the young man. "I imagine you've had a lot of experience."

"Sorry," said Harold, "but I'm saving myself up for the blonde in the green dress."

"You mean my fiancée," said the young man. "Perhaps we could all do it together."

"That wouldn't be clean," said Harold.

"By the way," the young man said, "my name is Roger. In the original German that means 'famous with the spear.'"

"Thanks anyway," said Harold.

* * *

"Hello, Dad," said Harold. "Guess where I am?"

"At your mother's nuptials, I suppose."

"It's more like an orgy," said Harold. "I'm getting depressed."

"I'm not surprised," said his father. "I'd be depressed myself."

"Couldn't you come out and give me moral support?"

"I don't believe I'd be properly appreciated, Harold."

"I don't know why not," said Harold. "I'm surprised Mother didn't invite you. I mean, it would fit the pattern."

"But I would have refused, Harold. One of your mother's weddings is enough for any man."

"I suppose it would be," said Harold.

"When is the ceremony?"

"Tomorrow afternoon. But I expect to be raped before then."

"The usual crowd, I take it."

"The house is crawling with perverts," said Harold. "I get enough of that at school."

"I told your mother not to send you there."

"Oh, I don't mind, really," said Harold. "It's just that it makes me horny."

"What does?"

"Being admired," said Harold. "Just being admired."

"Oh," said his father. "Well, that's natural enough. It's the cornerstone of sex, you might say."

"Yes, but some day I'm liable to give in, Dad, from being admired so much."

"Well," said his father, "it won't mark you for life if you do. Just be sure that you don't reciprocate."

"Don't be so liberal, Dad, it doesn't help things at all."

"I'm sorry, Harold. I'm only trying to be objective. Deep down, I'm a conservative, you know. Deep down, I'm really for cleanth."

Harold was silent for a moment.

"Are you there?" asked his father.

"How do you know about cleanth, Dad?"

"Why, that's my philosophy, Harold."

"I never heard you mention it before."

"It's not a fashionable view, Harold. You know it's a mistake to make public an unfashionable view."

"I'm glad you're for cleanth, Dad. Do you suppose we're talking about the same thing?"

"Let's hope so, Harold," said his father.

"Oh, I hope so, Dad," said Harold.

"Well," said his father, "to use one of your phrases, let it hang loose, Harold."

"I'll try," said Harold. "I really will."

* * *

Harold caught up with her in the hallway, just at her door.

"Are you really going to marry that faggot?" he said.

The blond girl looked vague. "Which one?" she asked. "There are so many around."

"The one named Roger," said Harold. "It means 'famous with the spear,' I'm told."

"Oh, him," said the blonde. "He's just my brother."

"He suggested a threesome," said Harold. "Do you go to bed with him often?"

"What a filthy idea."

"Why?" said Harold.

"Well, for one thing, he's queer."

"Are queers unclean?"

"I suppose that depends on whether or not you're queer."

"You mean it's all a matter of degree?" asked Harold.

"What is?" said the blonde, opening her door.

"Cleanth."

"Point of view, I should have said."

"From my point of view," said Harold, "I think it would be very clean if I went to bed with you. Or, rather, if you went to bed with me. Thanks for inviting me in."

"You still haven't guessed my name," said the blonde, blocking the doorway with a creamy arm.

"Gertrude," growled Harold.

"Don't be rude," said the blonde.

"Give me a hint," said Harold.

"Why should I?"

"You don't even want me to guess," Harold complained. "I can tell. Everybody I want rejects me. My only recourse is to therefore reject all who want me. But it's getting me down. At this rate I'll never lose my cherry."

"Who else do you want beside me?"

"No one right now," said Harold. "That's my problem."

"You're too possessive by far," said the blonde and closed the door in his face.

"Goddam White Goddess," said Harold.

*   *   *

"Mother, who's that blond girl?" asked Harold, looking out at the morning.

"Which girl is that?" asked his mother, gazing long at herself in her dressing table mirror.

"The one with the queer brother," said Harold. "His name is Roger."

"You mustn't pigeon-hole people, darling. How do you know he's queer?"

"He asked me to go to bed with him."

"Oh, I see. I supposed that must be taken as evidence. Do you find him attractive?"

"No, Mother, he just doesn't send me."

"Well, then, you see, he's probably not queer at all."

"It's his sister I'm interested in, actually."

"Oh, yes, the brunette."

"No, she was blond, last I noticed."

"She probably dyes it," said his mother.

"Please, Mother, it's important to me."

"Then she doesn't dye it. I hardly know the girl." His mother paused to take a sip from the martini at her elbow.

"Not even her name?"

"I suspect she's a friend of Sam's, love. She looks like a friend of Sam's, if it comes to that. Why don't you ask him? I really must dress." She turned from the mirror. "Do I look all right, darling? My hair?"

"Like a bride?" suggested Harold.

*   *   *

"I see you've commandeered my barn," said Harold, in the realms of art.

"Don't use such pretentious words, kid. They don't suit your youth."

"Where'd you pick up all this junk, anyway?" asked Harold, looking around at the piles of machinery.

"I forage, kid. I forage. But you didn't come out here to talk about art."

Harold squinted at his step-father-to-be. "Well, Sam, I'll tell you. I'd like a little information."

Sam squinted back. "What kind of information, kid?"

"There's this girl, Sam, whose name I'm trying to find out. She's a blonde, and yesterday she wore a green dress. It matches her eyes."

"What do you want to know her name for, kid?"

"If I guess it, she'll let me ball her," said Harold.

Sam shook his head. "I wouldn't want to be a party to the corruption of youth," said Sam.

"I'm already corrupt, I just haven't had any experience," said Harold.

"I've got to start thinking like a father," said Sam, wielding a welder.

"Enjoy my barn," said Harold.

"Don't be so possessive, kid. It doesn't suit your youth."

"Where you spill your seed, that ground is yours," said Harold in a philosophic tone. "Oh, and Mother asked me to tell you to get dressed. It's only an hour to the ceremony."

"Thanks, kid. Just as soon as I get this piece in place."

"How do you tell which ones are finished?" asked Harold.

*   *   *

"What a peculiar ceremony that was," said Roger.

"Outward form always must needs confirm inner truth," replied Harold.

"I adore lobster newburg, don't you?" said Roger, wielding a fork.

"It has it all over chicken and peas," agreed Harold.

"I think food is the second most fulfilling thing in the world," Roger continued.

"What's the first?" asked Harold, leaning against a pillar of the porch.

Roger reached out and drew a finger across the front of Harold's gray flannels. "Is that all you?" he asked. "I've been dying to know."

"Except for a few plastic grapes," said Harold. After a moment he added, "Don't do that while I'm eating, please."

"You don't like it?"

"I hate to mix my pleasures," said Harold.

"Then you do like it. Umm, I can tell. I could easily fall in love with you, you know."

"I'm more interested in your sister," said Harold.

"I don't have a sister," said Roger.

"Yes, you do," said Harold. "She's blond, and she has green eyes."

"Oh, you mean my fiancée," said Roger.

"She says you're her brother," said Harold.

"That's just a game she plays," said Roger.

"Could you tell me her name, old fellow?"

"You'd have to ask her," replied Roger. "She's fussy about that."

"God damn you all, anyway," said Harold.

*   *   *

"Mother, why don't you put down your glass for this one," said Harold, turning the film.

"Oh, all right," she said, draining it. "So long as it's the last picture. I shall rue the day I gave you your first camera, I know it."

"There's no harm in being a camera bug," said Sam. He gave Harold a wink of complicity, moving in on fatherhood fast. "He might even make a living out of it, some day."

"Oh, I hope not," Harold's mother demurred. "I never did meet a society photographer who wasn't a pansy."

"Move a little closer together," said Harold. "You'd think you were getting divorced instead of married," he went on to suggest.

"Let's not rush things, kid," said Sam.

"What do you mean, rush?" asked Harold's mother.

"Stand still for a second, Mother, and then you can argue."

"I was making a joke," said Sam. "You should never take me at face value," he added to Harold.

"I never take anything at face value," said Harold, "if I can help it."

*   *   *

"You don't believe in cleanth at all," said Harold. "You're a liar and a filthy slut."

"You do me an injustice," she replied, and her blond hair fell across her eyes.

"Corruption is all around me," Harold proclaimed. "Education has fallen into the hands of professional hypocrites, motherhood into the hands of amateur whores, art into the hands of former grease monkeys, and young love into the hands of apprentice perverts. And hope, hope has no name. I am disillusioned. To be disillusioned at my age is a crying shame."

"You guessed," said the blonde, sitting down on the stairs.

"What did I guess?"

"My name. My name is Hope."

"You're kidding," said Harold. "How fucking symbolic. Christ, are you ready for it?"

"Well," said Hope, "I suppose I did promise."

"I was talking to myself," said Harold.

"What do you mean?" asked Hope.

"I'm not ready for it," said Harold.

"Ready for what?"

"You," said Harold. "Christ, I'm not sure I'm ready for anything."

* * *

"Goodbye, Mother."

"Goodbye, darling. I'm so glad you came."

"It wouldn't have been the same without you," said Sam.

"Thanks," said Harold. "The same to you."

"Will you come again soon, darling?"

"Sure," said Harold. "Some weekend when you don't have any other guests."

"But I thought you were enjoying yourself," said his mother. "With that blond girl and her brother."

"Actually, she's his fiancée," said Sam.

"I don't understand modern marriage," said his mother. "All these peculiar sexual pairings."

"It puts a strain on the unity of the family," said Harold.

"What's that, dear?"

"Modern marriage."

His mother looked puzzled. "You're getting so sophisticated, darling."

"One of these days I'll take my place in society," said Harold.

"Just don't grow up too fast," said his mother.

"That's right, kid, let it hang loose," said Sam.

"Thanks for the advice, Dad," said Harold.

His mother dazzled them with one of her smiles. "I'm glad you two are getting along so well," she said.

"That's what frankness will do for you," said Harold. "Even if the cornerstone of civilization is hypocrisy," he added.

"Take care, darling," said his mother.

"Goodbye, Mother," said Harold.

*   *   *

"Hello, Spike," said Harold to his roommate.

"Oh, hi, Harold," said Spike, hurriedly zipping his fly. "So how was the wedding?"

"The opposite of filth is cleanth," said Harold.

"What does that mean, for God's sake?"

"Who knows?" said Harold. "That I still have my cherry, for one thing."

"Oh, pretty boring, you mean," said Spike.

"Yes," said Harold. "Pretty boring. But then, what can you expect? Happy families are all alike."

2 / Cherries

A Victorian gingerbread behemoth, the yacht club hunkered at the water's edge. It had been freshly painted in that spring of 1957. But no amount of pine green paint (nor even of white trim), Harold decided, would ever be able to eradicate its aura of general gloom.

Victoriana, on the whole, gave Harold the blues.

As he sat in the manager's office, however, he made use of his blues, disguising them to approximate the servility that Schranz so obviously expected of him. "The members of this club are important people," Schranz urged, his voice resonant with paranoia. "Very rich people, you understand, who expect to be waited on quickly and efficiently."

"Yes, I know," said Harold, forgetting servility. "With dispatch. My mother is rich. Not that she ever does anything with dispatch."

Schranz shook his head. "None of that is going to interest anyone around here," he said. "Familiarity is out. Do you read me? Absolutely out."

Harold, seeking similes, decided that Schranz had eyes like ice cubes melting in a blue bowl, cold but weak. "Yes, sir," he said.

"I don't care how rich your mother is, she's not a member of this club."

His mother was, however, at least partly to blame for Schranz. Her voice, Harold recalled, had been at its very sweetest. It always was when she had bad news to convey.

"Darling," she said, "I think you should get yourself a job for the summer. Don't you? And we'll hold off the delivery of the Ferrari until September."

The quality of Harold's silence had been steadfast.

"Say something, darling. You know I adore giving you presents. But I don't want to spoil you, my love." The concept of spoiling the child was not one with which Harold believed his mother to be well acquainted. His father's influence being therefore apparent, Harold called him collect in New York at the first opportunity.

"Hello, Harold, what's the trouble?"

"Oh, no trouble, Dad. I was just thinking I might get a job for the summer. I figured you could give me some advice."

"I was hoping that idea might cross your mind."

One thing Harold really liked about his Dad was that he never rubbed salt in your wounds.

"But I'd like to do something a little different, Dad. I mean not just pump gas or something."

"Different?" His father apparently did not approve of this choice of vocabulary.

"Yeah, I mean, you know, maybe being a forest ranger in the Northwest. Something like that."

"A forest ranger." There was a hint of relief. Harold immediately moved to give his father something more bizarre to consider, so as to make the fighting of forest fires appear actively appealing.

"Spike's brother had a cool job last summer," Harold ventured. "In Texas, artificially inseminating cows."

"Isn't that a little technical?" his father intimated after a pause.

"No, no, it's very easy. You wear long rubber gloves and just slide your arm up inside and break this plastic vial of bull sperm. You have to be sort of gentle and sexy about it, though, so the cow thinks she's getting a real screw."

"The scope of your learning often astonishes me, Harold."

"Well, when you go to a first-rate school you meet a lot of very bright people. You're just bound to pick up a good deal of miscellaneous information. I must say it's one of the things that makes me realize how lucky I am."

*   *   *

"I'm sure you think you know a hell of a lot about the world, with that background of yours," said Schranz. "But just don't go asserting your opinions around here."

"No, sir." Harold spoke very softly, without a hint of assertion.

"Now, I realize you're used to being waited on, rather than the other way around. That can make you better at your job, or it can make you lazy and impertinent. I've seen it work both ways. I hope you'll turn out to be one of the hard-working ones."

"I'll do my best, sir." Actually, as he had already explained at some length to his father, Harold did not feel psychologically equipped to succeed as a bar boy. His father, unsurprisingly, had disagreed, feeling that the development of a few new resources could do Harold nothing but good. In fact, he had come up with an unusually well-argued reply, even for a lawyer, marshaling an impressive number of moralistic clichés which, taken as a whole, revealed to Harold as never before the extent of his father's puritan belief in the development of character through suffering. It was a depressing revelation, although Harold had consoled himself with the knowledge that in this as in so many things, his own ability to comprehend the workings of man and this world far surpassed the experience of his years. Of course, putting such qualities of mind and heart to work on the tasks of a bar boy was a sheer waste of talent, but there was obviously no way around it.

It wasn't that Harold didn't want to work. He had thought of getting a job for the summer long before his parents had raised the issue. After all, he had reasoned, the real money in the family was his mother's, and at the rate she was spending it on liquor, to say nothing of solder for his stepfather the junk sculptor, Harold was clearly going to have to support himself some day. It had occurred to him that the summer between school and college was an appropriate, one might even say traditional, time to begin getting used to the rigors of adulthood, before that condition was thrust willy-nilly upon one.

Schranz, however, was not at all what Harold had had in mind in the way of a boss. Quite apart from being a mean-eyed Nazi bastard, the man was wearing a tan sharkskin suit, blue socks and black shoes.

"All right," Schranz said. "I guess that's enough do's and don'ts for the moment. Come on, I'll show you around."

He started Harold off by introducing him to Miss Agnes Hale. "She's been here twenty-seven years," Schranz noted, in the lady's presence, but without looking at her, "so don't give her any trouble. She even has me scared." And he parted his thin, very pink lips in a sudden leer, perhaps to indicate that he had made a joke.

Miss Agnes Hale was an ample woman with a prognathous jaw. Her grim visage, however, was suddenly sundered by a wide and genuine smile, like a shaft of sunlight in a thunder squall. "Call me Agnes," she boomed. "Everybody does. Any questions, just ask."

Harold felt less oppressed. Although it disturbed him to admit the fact (he saw it as a sign of vulnerability), Harold liked people who were nice to him.

"Hop to it," said Schranz, already several paces down the hall.

Harold caught up with him as he turned into the trophy room. Schranz ran a hand possessively down the side of a large glass case, leaving a definite smudge. "That one," he said, pointing to an ornate silver urn, "goes back to 1874."

"This is your first year at the club, isn't it, sir?" Like the voice of an inexperienced tenor seeking a high note, Harold's tone wavered uncertainly, rising toward servility only to fall back into insolence.

Schranz's nostrils tightened perceptibly. "Don't think that means you can put anything over on me, kid." He led the way back across the hall to a dimly lighted parlor. "I've been in this business twenty years."

"It must be tough work," said Harold, with only a minimal attempt at the obsequious.

"It has its problems," said Schranz. "Fresh kids among them."

Harold was on the verge of admitting to himself that he wasn't going to be able to handle Schranz, when the man's lips parted in another of his curious leers. He clapped Harold on the shoulder familiarly. "The old bags have sherry in here before their bridge lunch on Thursdays," he said.

"Most sherry glasses spill over easily," Harold remarked, drawing upon his mother's varied drinking habits to create an air of professionalism.

The fingers of Schranz's heavily freckled hand dug more deeply into Harold's shoulder. "I hope you aren't planning to filch a lot of hooch on the job, kid. You're underage and the only reason you're allowed to work here is because it's a private club. So no drinking on the premises or you'll get me in trouble with the Liquor Commission. And you wouldn't want to do that, would you, kid?"

"Certainly not, sir," said Harold, whose shoulder was beginning to tire. "Did you know, sir, that the word 'hooch' was derived from the Chinook?"

Schranz lifted his head abruptly. "The Chinese? What about the Chinese?" he asked with suspicion.

"No, no, it's an Indian tribe on the northwest Canadian coast."

A muscle in Schranz's cheek had a spasm. "Let me give you a piece of advice, kid. Nobody likes anybody who knows more than he does. If you want to get along in this world, always play it a little dumber than you actually are."

* * *

The interior of the club was paneled in dark wood. It gave Harold claustrophobia. He was tired of Schranz's advice and started leaving the "sir" off the ends of his sentences. At least no one else seemed to like Schranz either. The bartender, a roly-poly ex-vaudevillian named Danny O'Rourke, winked at Harold the moment Schranz's back was turned. And in the kitchen, the dishwasher discreetly made with the finger.

But it was not until the very end of Schranz's proprietary survey that Harold glimpsed some hope of the summer's salvation. Suddenly, when he least expected it, there was the glimmering of a new opportunity to achieve the loss of his cherry.

They were touring the second floor, where a number of bedrooms, lavish only in their use of chintz, were located. "Not often occupied," said Schranz. "Most guests are put up in the guest house across the way, where my suite is." Schranz seemed curiously proud to be rubbing backsides with the paying guests. Of course, given the long dingy corridor of rooms over the multiple garage where Harold was bunked out, Schranz probably had reason to be pleased with himself.

"Are those back stairs?" Harold asked, gesturing toward the shadowed recesses of the second floor.

For the first time, Schranz looked him straight in the eye. Harold was startled to see the man's face take on an expression of lustful complicity. Once again his freckled mitt descended upon Harold's shoulder. Good God, was he a pansy as well as a Nazi? Not that the combination was unknown.

But the man had a wife and child, Harold reminded himself, taking refuge in naïveté.

Schranz chuckled with a rusty sound. "That's where our two little waitresses sleep. Nice pieces, both of them, but if I catch you in their rooms I'll have your balls."

"I'd rather one of the waitresses did," said Harold, before he could stop himself.

But Schranz only laughed, full out, the sounds of atrophy even harsher than before. People who laughed seldom would do well to avoid it altogether, Harold decided. He was beginning to understand the man. Impertinence was acceptable only when disguised as smut, a revelation that seemed to Harold interesting if not especially useful. He wondered if it was the kind of educational discovery his father had quite expected him to make. But then, perhaps his father's main purpose was to expose him to the grating vulgarity of the real world, as opposed to the well-oiled vulgarity of the world in which he had grown up. But if that were the case, surely the decanting of bull sperm into the cunt of a Texas cow would have served even better.

Harold considered telling Schranz about the job he had almost had deep in the bowels of Texas, but decided to save it for a moment when a device to set the man drooling was more urgently required.

*   *   *

"My name is Harold," said Harold.

"My name is Stella," said Stella.

"Dallas?" asked Harold.

"Kowalski," said Stella.

"I'm Linda," said Linda, left out.

"Hello," said Harold. He looked back and forth at the two.

Linda was pretty in a commonplace way, blond and snub-nosed. Linda would do, Harold decided—almost anyone would do—but it was Stella he wanted, he thought. Stella had full breasts and fine, even teeth, very white. Her eyes were dark and her hair was dark. Besides, Harold liked her laugh, which was quite deep and rather dirty.

It was Stella he wanted, Harold was sure.

Since he was fifteen years old, Harold had worried about being a virgin. It had become a morbid subject with him for a time. Of course he knew it was an idiotic thing to worry about, since almost everyone had been one at some time or other. A lot of people still were virgins, from what he could gather, and there were even a few who seemed to cherish the state. When he was twelve, he had heard a friend of his mother's say that every six months she grew a new cherry and started all over again. Even then Harold had known she was joking, but there had been about the way she made this joke something curiously wistful, as though she really would have liked to be able to accomplish such periodic regeneration.

Part of the trouble, of course, was that almost every boy Harold knew contrived to give the impression that he'd already been laid several times. Most of them were lying, Harold was perfectly sure, but a few of them, he was just as sure, were telling the truth. It galled him extremely not to be in the vanguard of this fraternity. God knows, he had tried. At the junior prom he had managed to get two fingers up the sacred crack of Elsie Swindon, for a split second or two, and at the senior prom he'd actually persuaded that reckless child, Prudence Pearce, to jack him off in the bird sanctuary while he fondled her left breast (the only one he'd succeeded in getting out of her dress).

The most disturbing thing of all, though, was that with each day of continued virginity, he felt his confidence in himself draining away. At fifteen he had worried only about opportunity, not performance, but the more knowledge he gleaned about the subject—and he gleaned a great deal —the more convinced he became that the question of performance was, in fact, crucial. Harold told himself that, as with everything else in life, practice alone could make perfect, but he couldn't bear the thought of making a balls-up, so to speak, of his initial encounter.

Harold, and he was frank with himself about it, wanted to come on like Casanova from the start. To assist him in the achievement of this expert beginning, he had sought out the wisdom contained in five different sex manuals, two of them enhanced by positional drawings; in addition, he had pawed through piles of pornography. The manuals were extremely edifying, although he continued to be hazy about the proper function of the clitoris, a confusion engendered, no doubt, by having delved too deeply into the question of vaginal, as opposed to clitoral, orgasm.

He was eighteen years old. His patience was running out, as well as his time. Cherryhood was distinctly an unnatural state, and to enter college a virgin was out of the question. It had to be this summer, and Stella seemed the likeliest means. Not that he saw her as a mere object, of course.

"She's a very nice girl," said Harold. "And I'll bet she has marvelous thighs."

It took only the smallest indications of reciprocal interest from Stella—inflections of the voice and expressions of the eye not much above the subliminal level—to foster within Harold's mind and trousers a state of acute readiness for his initiation into manhood. He found it necessary to cover himself with his bar tray at the most extraordinary moments, leading him on one occasion to skitter across the dining room like a veritable fan dancer when Stella's smile roused his flesh to an untoward response.

Twice within a single week he was reprimanded by Schranz for failing to answer the call bell in the bar with sufficient rapidity. In both cases, Harold had been sitting at his regular post in the hall near the switchboard, daydreaming to such tremendous effect that, upon attempting to walk, he found it quite impossible to attain an upright posture without doing himself serious harm.

"Harold," said Harold, "this has got to stop."

In an attempt to gain control over the result if not the cause of such daydreaming, Harold cut a hole in the pocket of one of his three pairs of black chinos, making it possible to reach in and arrange matters less obtrusively. But the white waiter's jackets he wore did not reach low enough to hide what, even rearranged, was clearly a matter for private rejoicing. Moreover, the continual expansion and retraction of his eager flesh had produced a glandular confusion which in turn resulted in the almost perpetual leakage of pent-up love juices.

Harold was getting desperate.

From one of the two other bar boys, a high church Episcopalian aptly named Peter Paul, who had just completed his first year of divinity school, Harold sought spiritual guidance. Although Peter claimed to have mastered his own desires to a remarkable degree, and was awaiting the eventual release afforded by marriage with perfect equanimity and only an occasional wet dream, he was unable to explain the workings of his system of self-control in any way that Harold felt he could emulate, since faith in the efficacy of faith seemed to be the cardinal ingredient.

"Then ask Ricky for a blow job," Peter suggested, maligning the third of the bar boys that summer. Ricky was indeed limp of wrist and pretty as any girl, but Harold suspected that he was also, in his own line, as virginal as Harold in his. It all merely served to confirm Harold's worst suspicions as to the underlying cynicism of those who dedicated their lives to the church, most especially the Episcopalian church (his mother had made a fetish of collecting priestly wits of the Episcopalian persuasion). Harold decided to seek no further assistance, neither oral nor oracular, but to struggle with his problem alone, the crux of which was to get Stella alone with his problem.

Harold's efforts were hampered by his complicated work schedule. If he worked the long shift, nine to one and then six to eleven, Stella had disappeared by the time he was through for the day. If he worked the short shift, twelve-thirty to seven-thirty, then he got off while she was still working. He could have asked her to meet him at some time when they both were free, but fearing that she would say no to such a direct approach, Harold placed his hopes in conjunction through accident. It was better by far, he told his suffering body, to go slow and meet with eventual success than to go fast and meet with rebuke.

His only real opportunities to consort with her had come on the few evenings when the whole gang of them, Stella, Linda, Peter, Ricky and himself, had borrowed one of the club dinghies, without asking, and rowed from the peninsula to the main town across the harbor for a midnight pizza and an illegal drink. Illegal for all of them, that is, except Peter and Stella. Peter was twenty-three and Stella had just turned twenty-one, which meant that Harold's vodka and tonic had to be ordered by Stella. Peter might have ordered it, in fact Harold had suggested in no uncertain terms that he do so, but the sadistic bastard, like all those of religious persuasion, obviously regarded other people's sufferings as good for their souls and a tonic to his own self-esteem. Harold therefore had to suffer the pangs of indignity as well as the pangs of lust; and with the visible symbol of the first standing before him on the table, and the all too palpable reality of the second standing invisibly (he hoped) beneath it, he was reduced to a pitiful and altogether uncharacteristic silence.

Fortunately, Stella seemed to appreciate this reticence. She did not say too much herself, and the two of them sat quietly side by side (Harold had contrived that much at least, with Stella's apparent cooperation) while the others babbled like chimpanzees. They were usually crowded into a booth meant for four rather than five, so that Harold was unable to read very much into the pressure of Stella's leg against his—there simply wasn't any place else she could put it. Even if inadvertent, it was thrilling. And from time to time, unless his fevered imagination or hypersensitive flesh was over-reacting, she would give him a slight additional nudge with her knee, to mark her amusement at some particularly schoolgirlish exchange between Linda and Ricky.

It was after the fourth of these late evening outings, as they were returning to the dinghy, that Harold finally found within himself the courage (or perhaps merely a sufficient degree of desperation) to suggest a more intimate meeting. He slowed his pace, falling a few steps behind the others. Stella, walking beside him, slowed down as well.

"I'm getting a little tired of the Peacock Lounge," said Harold eloquently.

"Oh, I don't mind the Peacock so much. But I'm a little tired of all the chatter," Stella suggested, tactfully aiding and abetting his lust.

"That's really what I meant," Harold said, and took a deep breath. "Come take a walk with me tomorrow night. There's a nice place to sit on the rocks on the other side of the peninsula."

Stella turned to look at him. He couldn't see the expression in her dark eyes. "All right," she said. And her fine, even, very white teeth showed in a smile. She linked her arm through his and her breast bumped against him as they walked.

* * *

Harold had always liked breasts. American men were supposed to be hung up on breasts, of course, or so the sociologists said, but Harold didn't think his love of the mammary gland had been fostered simply by the dirty minds on Madison Avenue. Even if it had been, what the hell, how could there be anything wrong with liking breasts? They were, after all, in presence or absence, the most noticeable thing about women. What was beautiful in a face was a matter of taste, there was always some guy around to say that Marilyn Monroe was a pig. But nobody was going to deny she had big breasts. You could say you didn't like big breasts, but you couldn't say hers were small. It was not something open to debate.

Sometimes, in fact, Harold thought that one reason why he didn't feel more warmth toward his mother was because of her boring upper-class breasts, which were pear-like and rather widely spaced. Fortunately, though, his mother's love of artistic types had brought into Harold's ken, from the time of his earliest memories, a succession of beautiful women, many of them large-breasted and most of them given to low décolletage. A few of his favorites were even noted for abjuring that stifling invention, the bra. One of his earliest visual memories was of a pair of large creamy breasts, nestled within a dark green dress as they hung suspended over the top of his crib. In later years, through careful questioning, he had been able to establish that these visual stimuli of his infancy had belonged to none other than Madeleine Portland, film star of the Forties and now married to a South American cattle king. One of these days, Harold knew, he would turn on the boob tube and there would be Madeleine Portland displaying her breasts on *The Late Show*.

Stella, it turned out, had lovely breasts, and Harold liked them a lot. It wasn't just that they were large, because they weren't of extraordinary size. It was the way they were shaped that he liked. Full enough to be bouncy, but not so heavy as to sag. You could heft them and move them around, but they didn't hang there like over-ripe fruit. The flesh had a nice pliant firmness, a resilience under the fingertips that made his balls tighten just at the touch. The nipples were nice, too, not too pointy yet quick to harden, with a rosy halo of just the right size, neither too big nor too small. All in all, Harold thought that they were wonderful breasts. "Stella Dallas," said Harold, "you have beautiful breasts. I like them a lot."

"Kowalski," said Stella.

*   *   *

Harold was beginning to get nervous about it. After three weeks of sleeping with Stella, he still hadn't fallen in love with her.

"Why did you pick me, anyway?" he asked her one night in July.

"I didn't. You picked me."

"I suppose that means you would have picked someone else if you'd been given a chance."

Stella stretched, pulling her abdomen taut under Harold's hand. Her smile was mysterious. "Does it?" she said.

"David? Or Phil?" Harold's guilt at indulging in sex without love tended to express itself in terms of self-denigration, Harold had noticed.

"Why them?" Stella's smile went away.

"They're good-looking. Fun. Nice. Rich."

"You're good-looking. Fun. Nice. And rich, as if that had anything to do with it."

"No, my mother is rich," said Harold. "Besides, they're lifeguards. Lifeguards are glamorous, hadn't you heard? I'm just a bar boy."

"They do have better tans. There's only one trouble. They're neither nice nor fun, as I see them."

"Why not?"

Stella sighed. "Oh, it's silly of me, I guess, even to notice, but they don't even know I'm alive except in a sort of condescending how-are-you-today-serving-girl way. Summer waitress, future nurse. Big deal. They might go against their families' wishes to marry a chorus girl, but they wouldn't even sleep with a nurse."

Harold swallowed. His fishing expedition seemed to have come up with something from greater depths than he'd expected. "You mean they're snobs."

She stroked his head. "Yes."

"Maybe I am, too." Harold examined his conscience gingerly.

"No," she said, "you're not."

"I come from the same kind of background," Harold insisted.

"But you're not the same kind of person."

"Well," said Harold, "if you prefer bar boys to lifeguards, there's always Peter."

"Yes, but Peter's saving himself for true love, and I'm not the true-love type."

Harold wasn't quite sure what he was expected to reply and said nothing.

Stella watched his silence. She pursed her lips for a moment and then laughed. "Don't look so worried." She ran a finger down the length of his nose. "I don't want you to fall in love with me either, Hal. That would spoil everything."

"Would it?"

"Of course. It wouldn't be fun any more. It would be mostly a problem, everything considered."

"No, it wouldn't," said Harold, unconvinced but driven to romance.

Stella's hand moved over his thigh. She had very smooth hands. "Yes, it would," she said quietly, moving her long fingers. "Don't be such a sap."

"Well, I suppose," said Harold, as his cock stirred. "I really think I ought to fall in love with you, though. I mean it's only polite," he added, speaking truths under the guise of humor.

Stella laughed. "I'm glad you feel that way, at least a little. That's part of what makes you different from Phil."

"You talk a lot about Phil," said Harold, tracing a line from her throat to her belly with his forefinger. "Maybe you really like him best."

"No, I like him least. But he is the prettiest, except for you."

"Don't you think Ricky's pretty?"

"Do you?"

"No. He thinks I am, though."

"Has he made a pass at you?"

"Of course not. It'll be years before he gets up the cour-age to make a pass at anyone. I feel sorry for him. He prob-ably worries himself sick about it."

"Being queer?"

"No. Never having made it," said Harold, harkening to all too recent memories.

"Did you worry about never having made it? Before me?" Stella looked amused.

"Sure," said Harold, with a show of bravery. "You must have realized how nervous I was that first night."

"No. Were you nervous? A little over-anxious, yes. I wasn't sure you'd keep all the way back from those rocks."

"I wasn't sure, either," said Harold, happy at being able to laugh.

"But I truly wouldn't have guessed it was your first time, if you hadn't told me later."

"Hell," said Harold, wounded, "and I thought I'd im-proved since then."

Stella laughed and pulled him down to her. "I assure you, you have," she said, stroking his back. "But you weren't bad to start with."

"Are you sure I'm not supposed to fall in love with you?" asked Harold, raising his head and looking into her eyes.

"Positive," said Stella, pushing the hair back out of his eyes. "I'm too old for you, anyway."

"Like hell," said Harold, and began to kiss her, her eyes to shut them, her mouth to open it, her nipples to make them stiffen, her belly to make her move her hips. There was nothing like sex, Harold had found, to stop you from worry-ing about love.

*　　*　　*

David and Phil, coming back from one of the parties they went to almost every night, were drunk.

David was drunker than Phil and carried a bottle of scotch under his arm. Harold ran into them returning to his room over the garage at two in the morning. "Is she a good lay?" asked David, climbing the outside stairs to the dormitory.

"Who?" said Harold.

"What's her name. Stella?"

"How should I know?" said Harold.

"Well, then it's the other one," said David, missing a step and clutching the rail. "What's the other one called, Phil?"

"Linda," said Phil, grabbing the bottle of scotch.

"Linda," David repeated. "Is Linda a good lay?"

"I haven't any idea," said Harold.

David turned at the top of the steps. His tanned face was brightly flushed under the light of the single bare bulb by the door. "Look, don't tell me you aren't fucking either of them," he said. "I know better than that. Let me see your cock. I can tell a cock that's been fucking."

David leaned back against the screen door. Harold paused one step from the top.

"Shut the hell up," said Phil. "You'll wake Schranz."

"Who the hell cares," yelled David. "I don't care who I wake up. I want to know if Hal baby is getting it off good." He leaned forward and patted Harold on the shoulder. "We gotta take care of our own, isn't that right, Phil?"

"You must be thinking of somebody else," said Harold.

David put on a face of severity. "No, I'm talking about you, Hal baby." He gathered himself together and waggled his finger in Harold's face. "You mustn't go getting soft on the kitchen help, boy. It won't do. It won't do at all. Next thing you know we'll have a pantry wedding. That's bad form. Terrible form," said David.

*   *   *

"Twice I've been married," said Danny O'Rourke, as he polished his mahogany bar. "And two times divorced. Then I almost got married a third time, but I said to myself, Danny boy, what hasn't worked twice isn't going to work the third time either. Things run in threes, you know, and I'd have to get through a third to arrive at a fourth. The fourth might bring a change of luck, but then it might not. And it's not worth a third one like the first two just to get on to the fourth. I'm too old. Of course, a man like me, if I want it regular, I almost have to get married, or pay for it maybe. I give it to them better than most in the sack, but I don't look like much on the street, if you know what I mean. A boy like you, though, Harry, why with your looks they'll come crawling on their knees to you, just begging for it. Every man thinks he wants a woman for his own, but believe me, Harry, it's better by far to have a whole harem that's only half yours. That way you get the quim without the quarreling, as it were. Take it from me, Harry, don't get too serious about any particular one, no matter how nice she seems."

"I wasn't planning to," said Harold, cracking his knuckles.

"You stick to that, Harry, and you'll be a happy man," said Danny O'Rourke.

"Are you happy here, kid?" asked Schranz, sneaking up from the rear and clapping a hand on Harold's shoulder. Harold turned from his contemplation of the harbor, filling with boats for Race Week. The summer was going. "Yes, sir," said Harold.

Schranz looked down at him from his one-inch advantage. He parted his lips pinkly. "Nothing like a little nooky to keep a man content, is there, kid?"

"I beg your pardon?" said Harold.

"I really like you, kid," said Schranz. "You're a cool one. Not like those other two fairies."

"You watch out for that man," said Agnes. "He's got it in for you, some way."

"Oh, I get along with Schranz all right," said Harold. "I even think he likes me."

"So he may, but watch out even so. He's a strange, jealous man."

"Oh, come off it, Agnes, you sound like a fortuneteller. I didn't think they believed in that stuff down in Maine."

Agnes looked at him over the top of her half glasses. "You leave my home state out of it. And if you won't watch out for yourself, watch out for your girl, then."

"Stella?" said Harold.

"She's your girl, isn't she?" said Agnes.

*   *   *

The night was very hot and gummy. There was not even a breeze from off the water, and although the windows to Stella's room were open, the curtains did not stir.

It was no night for rolling about. They made love slowly and quietly, without speaking. The sky was heavy with summer silence. Later there would be storms, and rain. Harold could feel it on his skin, between his shoulder blades, that it would be a night for rain.

The pounding on the door of Stella's room came with the suddenness of late summer thunder, startling yet subconsciously expected.

"Open up," Schranz bellowed out of the night, and pounded on the door.

Harold's heart leaped and pounded in answer. He could feel Stella stiffen beneath him. But he refused to hurry. Gently, he disengaged himself.

"I'm going to give you twenty seconds to open this door and then I'm going to use my key," Schranz said in a rising voice.

Harold got to his feet, pulled the sheet up from where it dangled over the foot of the bed, covered Stella and reached for his trousers, his erection falling to the crisis.

"Here I come, ready or not," said Schranz, in a perverted echo of childhood games.

As he came in the door, Harold zipped up his fly.

"Well, well, what do you know, making fucky," said Schranz. His pink lips lingered wide in one of his dangerous smiles.

"You have no right to come in here," said Harold quietly.

"I thought I'd just watch for a while," Schranz suggested in a conversational tone.

Harold glanced at Stella, who had closed her eyes.

"That sheet is ruining my view, honey," said Schranz.

"Get out of here," said Harold.

"No, kid. I think you'd better get out. Unless you're prepared to give me a show."

"I'll get you fired, Schranz. Somehow, I don't think the House Committee would approve."

"I'll have your balls first, kid." Schranz's voice went up a notch.

"What's your problem, Schranz? You seem to be hung up on my balls," said Harold, with a calm he did not feel.

"You finish dressing, kid. I want you out of here in five minutes. And from now on this room is off limits. You read me?"

"What difference does it make to you?" Harold's voice began to shake slightly.

"I made a rule, kid. Too many people know you're breaking it. Understand?" Schranz suddenly grinned. "On the other hand, you could just say I don't want anybody around here having more fun than I do."

"Bastard," said Harold.

"Get dressed, kid. I mean it. Out!" Schranz pointed to the door.

Harold reached for his shirt.

"That's more like it. And remember, five minutes. You should thank me for letting you have that much time." He paused, his pink lips apart. "It's enough for you to get your rocks off, if she knows her business." Schranz looked briefly down at Stella and turned toward the door.

Stella opened her eyes. "I want that key to my room," she said, in a low, clear voice.

Schranz looked back at her. "Do you, now? Well, you aren't getting it."

"Then I'll leave," Stella said.

Schranz shrugged. "So? There are always more of your kind around." Schranz walked out of the room and shut the door behind him.

Harold looked at Stella. She stared at the ceiling. "I'm sorry," he said in a muted voice. His anger and his sense of helplessness canceled one another out.

"It's not your fault."

"Yes, it is. Agnes warned me to be careful. I should have listened to her."

"It doesn't matter."

Harold moved toward the bed. "Stella, I—"

"Let's not talk about it tonight, Hal." She turned her head on the pillow and looked at him. Her dark eyes were masked. "Okay?"

Harold hesitated. "If that's what you want."

"It is." She gave him a quick smile and held out her hand. Harold knelt on the bed and kissed her cheek.

"I don't like to leave you," he said.

"I know."

"See you tomorrow."

"Yes," said Stella. "Tomorrow."

There was no sign of Schranz in the halls. Harold went outside, and down to the dock. He walked out to the end and stood watching the slow-moving water for a long time. At last, the thunder began, with a tremendous crash, and lightning rippled down the sky in sheets. It was three o'clock in the morning.

*   *   *

"You seem gloomy today," said Danny O'Rourke, cutting lemons and limes.

"That's right," said Harold.

"Ah, and I'll wager it's woman trouble," said Danny, trotting out his brogue.

Harold shrugged. "In a way," he said. He didn't want to talk about it, really.

"They're only good for one thing," said Danny. "And half the time they're not worth much at that."

"That's a lot of crap," said Harold.

Danny's round face flushed, and he looked down abruptly at his cutting board.

"I'm sorry," said Harold. "Schranz busted in on me and Stella last night. Not at a very good moment either."

"The filthy bugger," said Danny, with no trace of brogue. "The miserable bastard."

"Yes." Harold wondered what Stella was doing. He was afraid, almost, to see her.

"I'll give you a drink," said Danny.

"Thanks, Danny. A Bloody Mary, I guess." He'd been breaking Schranz's rule about drinking all summer, with Danny's assistance. It was a special pleasure to do so this morning.

"Do you like life, Danny?" Harold asked.

Danny looked up in surprise. "Well now," he said. "There have been times I have and times I haven't, but I seem to be bloody well stuck with it. That's a bad thing to bother your head about, you know, especially when you're young. Drink up and forget about it."

Harold had taken only one sip when the bell rang at the front desk. "Oh, shit," he said. "It's probably Schranz."

"Take a big gulp of your drink, then."

Harold did as he was told.

"All right, go along now. The rest of it'll be here underneath," said Danny, removing the glass from view.

Harold headed for the front desk. Schranz's office, next door, was empty. "What's up?" he asked Agnes.

She did not smile. "Stella is leaving."

"What do you mean—leaving?" Harold was stunned. And yet he had known, without knowing. It was why he had been afraid to see her.

"She's quit. She's leaving for good."

"But—but why?"

"I thought you'd know that." Agnes was all thunder and no sunlight.

"No, not really. Well, I mean—" Harold paused. "Where's he this morning?" he asked, gesturing to Schranz's office.

"It's all right, he's in his rooms."

"He gave us a pretty bad time last night. You were right about him. But I didn't know Stella was that—oh, hell."

"I warned you, Harry Hoskins."

"I know. It's all my fault."

"Perhaps." Agnes began to relent. "Even so, he has no business interfering with people when they're not working."

"Where is she, Agnes?"

"In her room, packing."

Harold took the stairs two at a time. The door to Stella's room was closed. Harold knocked, feeling strange and far away.

"Who is it?"

"It's me."

"All right. Come in."

Harold opened the door. There were two suitcases on the bed. Stella hardly looked at him. "Hello," she said.

"Why are you leaving?"

"I have to."

"Were you fired?"

"No. But I can't cope with Schranz."

Harold stood halfway across the room, watching her long deft fingers folding clothes and placing them in the suitcases.

"Did he come back here last night or something?" Harold's knees felt weak.

"No. I just can't face him, that's all, with that smirk of his. There are only three weeks left and I've saved most of what I've earned. Anyway, I'm tired."

"I'll leave, too," said Harold.

"Why?" She continued folding her clothes.

"Well, I mean, I could come see you," said Harold, and had a vision of himself driving at twilight in a strange town by a river.

Stella turned and looked fully at him. Her eyes were puffy. She gave a small smile and then, shaking her head, looked away again. "There's no point, Hal."

"I want to," he said, convincing himself.

"No, Hal." She gave him a quick look, her eyes assuring him that she meant what she said. "Please don't."

Harold moved across to her. He turned her around and put his hands on her waist. "I want to," he repeated.

She put her hands on his and removed them from her waist. "I said no, Hal. I meant it."

"But why?" He felt a childish insistence growing in himself.

"There's no future in it, for either of us. I know that sounds corny, but it's true. If you don't know it yet, I do. It would just make me sad, Hal."

Harold was silent for a moment. He felt thoroughly confused. "I love you," he said. But it was almost a question.

Stella gave a short laugh, which made his heart jump. "Oh, come on, don't do that now. You know you don't. You don't even know what it is."

"Maybe I'm just beginning to find out." Harold's voice shook, from uncertain emotions.

She faced him again, put a hand on his arm and looked straight into his eyes. "Look, Hal, I like you. Very much. We had fun. Now don't spoil it. There can't be anything more, and if you try you'll just spoil what there is. So don't." Her voice was kind but absolutely firm, as though she were talking to a patient.

Harold could find nothing to say. She continued to look at him. "Okay?" she asked.

"Even if Schranz had come back here last night, you wouldn't tell me, would you?"

Something closed and opened again in her eyes, like the shutter in a camera. "No," she said, and turned back to her packing.

Harold realized that he didn't want to know, if indeed it were true. "Will you at least give me your address?"

She went on with her packing. "No."

"Well, I could find it, anyway, if I went to Lowell, just by looking in the phone book."

"Yes, you could."

"Well, then, I'll see you."

She straightened up again. Her shoulders rose and fell in a sigh. "I'm not going to argue," she said, turning around once more. "You say that, but you know you won't. And please don't come charging around just to prove that I'm wrong."

Harold suddenly felt tears prickling at the backs of his eyes. He didn't know why they were there, but they were.

Stella noticed at once. She smiled and tousled his hair. She put a hand on each of his shoulders and leaned toward him. "Don't," she said. "I never expected anything else. It's fine, just as it stands. Now give me a hug and go away."

"I'm sorry," Harold said, as the tears spilled over onto his cheeks. He felt about eight years old. Maybe nine.

"What for?"

"I don't know," said Harold, and, truly, did not.

"Silly boy." Stella put her arms around him, hugged him close, and said, "Go, go, go." She gave him a final smile and a push. Then she turned away.

Harold moved two steps toward the door and stopped.

"Goodbye, Stella Dallas," he said.

Stella did not say Kowalski.

3/Business

ONE April morning in the early 1960s a buzzer sounded in the cheapest room of a small hotel on the Île de la Cité, in the first arrondissement of Paris, France. It was not yet ten o'clock and Harold was still asleep. During the past few days he had been sleeping a great deal. It was the best way he knew to keep from thinking, better even than hashish, of which he had a small remaining supply, originally procured at a café in the Algerian quarter behind the Place de la République and now sequestered in a pair of worn-out socks in the upper drawer of the much scarred bureau which constituted one of the four pieces of furniture in his narrow room.

Harold was avoiding a decision.

Soon, though, today, tomorrow, this week at least, he would have to come to terms with reality. The alternatives were few. He was coming to the end of the funds he had raised through the sale of his Ferrari (the smartest prep school graduation present ever requested by a potential dropout, affording Harold not only three years of capitalist pleasure but an additional year of anti-establishment fervor in the back streets of Europe).

His parents had refused, piously, to contribute further funds to what they saw as his self-destruction, but they had indicated their willingness to supply a return ticket to America if he would agree either to go back to college or get a job. His father had felt constrained to point out, however, that it was possible to purchase a ticket whose value could be reclaimed only by the purchaser, even though issued in the name of another, thus frustrating Harold's vague plans for the redeployment of the approximately two hundred and fifty dollars involved.

But Harold did not feel he was ready either for America or an American job, and any return to the world of formalized learning he dismissed out of hand. Equally disagreeable was the thought of searching for a legitimate job in Paris. Perhaps, in fact, that was the most unpleasant prospect of all, one quite impossible to square with the indefinable romance of the City of Light. Among a certain kind of young American, the love of Paris amounts to a mild disease, like measles or chicken pox. Harold, a voracious reader, had been exposed early, through the literary works of the Lost Generation. They did not have quite as profound an effect on him as on those who had read them right after the war, but they had prepared the way for other, more contemporary influences. In Harold's case the most singular of these was *À Bout de Souffle*, Jean Luc Godard's tender paean to anarchy, which had opened in America under the title of *Breathless* the previous spring. Harold had seen it eight times in less than a month and knew it by heart, shot for shot. There were moments now in Paris when Harold knew he was Lazlo Kovacs, and for Lazlo Kovacs the seeking of a job in the city of Paris could not be a serious thought.

A third possibility, more in Lazlo's line, was to become an additional link in his friend Jean-Pierre's lengthening chain of amateur smugglers, who passed hash from hand to hand around the globe, westward from Beirut. Harold suspected, however, that heroin was also involved, and so was held back by a lamentable combination of cowardice and common sense that often conspired to save his neck.

None of these various alternatives therefore held much appeal while even a few Ferrari francs remained to him. And since wakefulness simply meant going over the same ground again in his head, without reaching any conclusion, he greatly wished, on this particular morning in April, that the buzzer had not sounded, or at least would sound no more.

But it came again, three short sharp burrs of noise that worked their way insistently beneath the outer skin of his sleep. Neither the buzzer system nor the concierge, Harold had come to learn, had survived the Second World War to be ignored by a mere paying guest, especially one who paid so little—on the contrary, he was expected to make a special effort to preserve the yellowed whorls of Madame's forefinger from additional friction.

Three rings meant that there was a phone call for him. There was no one, Harold was quite sure, with whom he presently wished to speak. But the nerves in his legs had begun to quiver with tension, urging the movement of muscle and bone. Harold was slept out and he knew it.

Before the buzzer could again assault his dawn sensibilities, he leaped naked from the bed and opened the door wide enough to yell, "Oui, oui, j'arrive," to Madame two floors below. He pulled on a jersey, a pair of jeans, and stepped barefoot into his loafers. As he crashed down the last few steps, Madame Simone scowled in greeting and began to scream at one of the maids, who had apparently committed the unpardonable error of carrying out the request of a guest without consulting Mrs. Simone Legrée, as she was affectionately known to the hotel's small cadre of Americans.

Harold held the receiver tight against one ear and put a finger in the other. "Oui?" he said. "Hello?"

An American voice replied. It was an exceedingly suave voice and not one that Harold immediately recognized. "Hello, is that you, Harold?"

"Yes. Who's this?"

"It's Charles Boardman."

"Oh. I see." Harold was tempted to hang up. Charles Boardman, sometimes called Charley-O by former class-mates, was a partner in his father's law firm. It boded ill.

"You needn't sound so distressed, Harold. Your father did suggest I look you up and give you a decent meal. But I promise not to lecture you. In fact, your father didn't even ask me to."

"He probably just assumed you knew what was required of you," said Harold, without any attempt to sound as though he were making a joke.

"Well, if so, he assumed wrong. Are you free for lunch? I'd suggest this evening, but I've got to take some friends of friends to the Tour d'Argent or some such tourist trap."

"Yeah, I'm free for lunch." Harold decided to accept, for the sake of the food. Then he could have just a bowl of soup for supper and save a couple of francs.

"Is there any place in particular you'd like to go?"

Harold considered suggesting the Tour d'Argent, just to be shitty. But he didn't want to go someplace where there'd be whole rafts of Americans any more than Charley-O seemed to. "There's a very good small place on the rue Monsieur-le-Prince," said Harold. "Not many tourists."

"So long as the food is good."

"Can you find the street?" Harold asked.

"I believe so." Charley-O sounded amused. "Why don't we meet at the café on the corner of the Boulevard St. Germain and the Carrefour de l'Odéon," he suggested.

* * *

The café on the corner of St. Germain and the Carrefour abused its choice location with what Harold believed to be the most unpleasant complement of waiters in all of Paris. When slighted, as they saw it, in the matter of tips, they became absolutely manic. One had actually chased Harold for almost a block, brandishing a metal tray and screaming his hatred of youth and foreigners, especially young Americans. It was an experience that had very nearly brought a flush of patriotism to Harold's breast, but not quite.

Charley-O was already there. Harold hardly recognized him, however. Dressed in a continental suit, very expensive and fashionable, he didn't match up with Harold's memories of him in an American setting. Since his parents' divorce, Harold hadn't seen much of Charles Boardman, but outside of a mild addiction to unusual ties, there had never seemed anything overtly chic about him.

Yet today he looked more like an Italian movie director than anything else. Harold's acquaintance with Italian movie directors was actually rather limited, outside the pages of *Sight and Sound* (the only one he had in fact met affected the turtleneck-and-leather-jacket look), but it was a designation that conjured up in his mind a certain kind of person, one whose rather flashy image Mr. Boardman seemed to have adopted for the occasion. He even came on like a supposed Italian movie director, giving a slight bow as he stood and extended his hand.

"Hello, Mr. Boardman," said Harold.

"How are you, Harold? I'm delighted you were free."

"Very free," said Harold.

The waiter was his old enemy, but either he didn't recognize Harold or did recognize potential largesse in the person of Charley-O. At any rate, he retreated to fetch a vermouth cassis for Boardman and a pernod for Harold without even the arching of an eyebrow in salute to past moments of spleen. Charley-O ordered in excellent, if somewhat pretentious, French. Harold's French was reasonably coherent and efficacious, but he had no interest in making it anything more than that: he ran off at the mouth sufficiently in English, as it was. Since he couldn't think of anything more interesting to say, however, he complimented Charley-O on his accent.

Charles Boardman smiled. "Well, I spent quite some time

in Paris before the war. In fact, I did some graduate work at the Sorbonne. That was before I decided to go into law."

"Really," said Harold very flatly.

He looked across the boulevard. A girl he knew slightly, a very pretty blonde named Pam whom he thought it would be nice to lay except that she was looking for French cock, it being Paris and she American, was just going into a cheapish restaurant across the way where Harold had sometimes eaten until all but the very cheapest places became too expensive for him. He would have liked to go join her. Even though she was taking a course at the Sorbonne herself, she had charmed Harold by accepting at face value his reasons for having abandoned the more formal routes to knowledge.

Charley-O was touching his arm, lightly. "Don't take offense," he said.

Harold looked across at him.

"I wasn't trying to tout education as such. Really, I quite understand how you feel about things, Harold. If I were a member of your generation, I would probably have left too."

Harold was doubtful. He had come to regard with increasing skepticism the protestations of understanding offered by anyone over twenty-five. Such understanding was invariably coupled with equally sincere protestations of amazement once it came to light that Harold had departed on the verge of completing three full years, and had simply failed to appear for his June exams. It was pointed out to him, as though he were too dumb to realize the fact, that if he had at least taken his exams he would have been in a much stronger position should he ever choose to return to the ivied halls.

"Well, that's all right," Harold would say, "I plan to grow up to be a bridge-burner, anyway."

In later years, when dropping out would become far more common and, in some quarters, be regarded as both a form of social responsibility and a sign of superior intelligence, Harold would receive perhaps more than his just share of adulation at having been a pioneer in this small but important area of rebellion against the American way of death. But sitting in Paris while John Kennedy created the Peace Corps, brought culture to the White House and made going to Harvard even more of a coup than before, there was little question that Harold seemed out of step with his time. He was well aware of the fact, and although he suspected that he might merely be ahead of his time, the whole question, at least as a conversational gambit, depressed him. He was constantly finding it necessary to defend his own actions, which he did badly, while being denied the opportunity to attack the kind of education (supposedly the *ne plus ultra* of its sort) that he had been receiving, which he did rather well.

Thus he was not about to lay himself open very wide to Charles Boardman's "understanding." "Really?" he said, feeling vaguely repetitive. "You mean you wouldn't want to be a lawyer today?"

Charley-O lifted his vermouth cassis, which had just arrived. "To Paris," he said.

"To Paris," said Harold with feeling.

"I would probably want to become a lawyer in the long run, even today," Boardman went on. "Perhaps even more so today. But I can see a good deal of value in taking some time off to review the facts, given the incredible complexity of today's world."

Harold hated givens. So many things that people accepted as givens both could and should be thrown out the window as far as he could see. "I'm not just taking time off, Mr. Boardman," he said, in a definite attempt at rudeness. "There's only one reason for education, and that's to learn how to think. Most formal education is designed to prevent you from thinking, or at least it has that effect. I already know how to think. I see no point in memorizing mere facts to throw back at some absentee professor on an exam. Facts are always available, you know, assuming you can use a

library. Anything I want to find out, I can teach myself."
Growing angry, he shut up.

"I see," said Boardman, who clearly didn't like what he saw.

To avoid a lecture, Harold decided to be disarming. "Now that we've clearly established that I'm arrogant and irresponsible," he said, "can we talk about something else?" And he threw in a smile for good measure.

Boardman did not answer immediately. He was looking at Harold intently. "You still have that extraordinary smile," he said rather suddenly.

Harold, himself disarmed, put down his pernod without drinking. "What?"

"I remember the first time I saw you, Harold, shortly after I joined the firm. You must have been about five or six. You had the most winning smile I had ever seen. I was very struck by it."

"Oh, well." Harold shrugged.

"You shouldn't disdain beauty, Harold. It's far too rare."

Harold remembered something interesting about Charley-O. He was supposed to be queer, even though he was married and had children. Harold's parents had had an argument about it once, a few years ago, when his mother had spotted Charley-O at the ballet with some young man. When she got home and made some comment about seeing Charles and "another of his kept boys," Harold's father had replied curtly, "You don't know that." Harold's mother had insisted that she did know, she knew at least one young man who had been to bed with him. And then Harold's father had made some acid remarks about the bloody lying little fag artists his mother insisted on hanging around with. It was at that point that they had realized Harold was sitting fifteen feet away in the study and had said no more.

Harold looked at Charley-O again. It was hard to tell. Except maybe for the suit. Dirty old men always wore continental suits, at least the ones who liked boys. The ones who liked little girls were given to rumpled tweeds or soiled gabardine. At least it amused Harold to assume so.

"How's Nancy?" Harold asked, by way of being misleading.

Nancy was the eldest of Charley-O's three children, the same age as Harold. Harold had sometimes taken her to parties when they were in their early teens, but he hadn't seen much of her lately.

"She's fine," Boardman replied. "You haven't dated her in some time, have you?"

"No," said Harold. "We never really managed to get up much interest in one another." Actually, Nancy had once shown a rather fervent interest in Harold, when they were both about eleven. She'd asked him to show her his cock one day. That was the word she'd used, too. "Harold, show me your cock, will you?" she'd said. Harold had refused, out of sheer shock. Nancy had then offered to undress so he could see what she was like, "all over" as she had put it, with a sudden retreat into coyness. But Harold had spurned even this reciprocal offer. Since Nancy didn't have any breasts yet, he figured he had more to show than she did. She would therefore be getting the best of the deal, which he couldn't allow.

"Do you have a girl here in Paris?" Boardman asked.

"No," said Harold. "I'm on the lookout, but she has to be not only beautiful but rich. And willing to spend her money on me, to keep me in the style I deserve. It narrows the field a lot."

"I take it you could, shall we say, be better off financially?" Boardman's casualness was rather studied; perhaps that was what he was supposed to find out for Harold's father.

"That's true." Harold picked up his pernod. He was undecided about how specific he should be. If he painted a picture of sufficient bleakness, the tale carried back to New York by Charley-O might persuade his father to send along some cash after all, just to keep Harold alive long enough to give him a chance to reform. On the other hand, it might be wiser to let his father think he could take care of himself. If it was obvious that he couldn't take care of himself, then his father, who was not often given to pity, would merely have some new ammunition on his side.

"Your father wondered if you'd sold your cameras," said Charley-O.

Harold made a face. "He really doesn't understand much of anything, does he? Of course I haven't sold my cameras. Any other questions?"

Boardman appeared to be suppressing a smile. "How are you planning to support yourself, then?"

"I thought I might become a hustler," said Harold. "Put my winning smile to good use."

As in many situations where he had no clear idea of what to say, Harold had opted for flipness. But why he had chosen to be flip about this particular subject at that particular moment, he couldn't have said, except that it probably was caused by recalling his mother's comments about Charley-O. Jean-Pierre, of course, had been advocating that line of work for some time, but it wasn't one that appealed to Harold or one that he thought he'd be particularly good at.

For his part, Charley-O looked first startled, then curious, and finally wary. Harold was surprised at how easily he could read Boardman's expressions. "Have you had any, uh, experience?" Boardman asked.

"No," said Harold. "But it doesn't require any special skills, does it? I come with built-in tools of the trade."

Charley-O's eyes flicked up and down, briefly, as though he were trying to restrain himself from examining Harold's crotch.

"Do you think I'd be a success?" asked Harold rather nastily.

"I have no idea, Harold." Charley-O seemed confused. "Is that a serious question?"

"What do you mean, serious?"

Charley-O studied him for a moment. "I mean are you playing games with me?" Boardman appeared to regain his assurance.

"No." Harold spoke flatly.

Once again Boardman regarded him silently. "And you are seriously considering becoming a male prostitute?" he asked after a moment.

Harold shrugged. "Sure." The term "male prostitute" was somehow unsettling, in a way the word "hustler" was not, but Harold wasn't about to give away any points at this stage. "Why not? You're the one who mentioned my smile."

Boardman chuckled. A slight smile, of the inscrutable variety, lingered on his lips. "Yes, that's true," he said. "Shall I be your first customer?"

This was not a tack Harold had expected. Even if his mother was right and Charley-O was queer, Harold would have thought that his side of the game would have consisted of disguising the fact.

"What's the matter, Harold, having second thoughts?"

Harold hesitated. Boardman had managed to speak this last sentence in such a way that it was difficult to tell exactly what was meant by it. It was clearly a goad, but there was no hint as to whether he was trying to get Harold to commit himself further because he was actually interested in purchasing the use of his flesh—or whether he was getting ready to pull the rug out from under him, by disavowing interest once Harold had thoroughly implicated himself.

"How much are you willing to pay?" asked Harold, deciding, like a good American boy, that a strict adherence to commercialism would eventually obliterate any moral qualms.

"How much do you think you're worth?" Boardman was very calm.

"That depends on how much you want me," said Harold, and felt pleased with himself.

Boardman sat impassively for a moment. Then he broke out in a conspiratorial smile. "This game could become positively exhausting," he said.

Harold leaned back in his chair, stretching his legs out in front of him. "Oh, I'm beginning to enjoy myself."

"How adolescent of you," said Boardman, giving, for the first time, some indication of annoyance. Nevertheless, he glanced at Harold's thighs.

"I'm just interested in finding out how much I could make as a hustler," said Harold. "I mean, whether it's actually a viable profession."

"I'm afraid my lack of knowledge on the economics of the question is quite profound," said Boardman.

"Really? I once heard mother talking about you and what she referred to as one of your kept boys."

Boardman's face tightened ominously. Harold hoped he hadn't gone too far. He took a sip of pernod to steady his nerves.

"Your mother is not always the most reliable source of information." Boardman's voice remained even.

Harold nodded. "That's true. In fact, my father disputed her statement."

"Oh? What did he say?"

Boardman appeared to realize immediately that this degree of curiosity was less than cool. "The relationship between your father and mother always struck me as somewhat bizarre," he added quickly, in an obvious attempt to erase one indiscreet remark with another.

Harold resisted the bait. At any rate, it was difficult to take issue with statements with which you agreed. "I think my father said, 'You don't know that,' something along those lines. There was an implication that proof was needed before a verdict of guilty could be brought in. Or maybe that he just didn't want to face the facts." Taking another sip from his pernod, Harold looked straight at Boardman.

Charley-O returned the gaze quite levelly. "That's very interesting," he said after a moment and looked out at the moving traffic. "I can't really say what you would be able to command from the average customer," he said, speaking quietly but with no trace of nervousness. "For my part, however, I would be willing to offer you fifty dollars." He glanced back at Harold, smiling slightly. "As a gesture of friendship, and to show my support for youth, as it were."

Harold was quite certain that Boardman was no longer playing a game, though he could not have said exactly when the transition to reality had taken place. But he himself felt suddenly unreal. Game-playing was one thing. He could handle that, perhaps better than most. But reality, at least this particular one, gave him pause.

"Fifty dollars," he echoed.

"Yes. That should keep you going for a while. As much as a week, perhaps."

"Sure," said Harold. "At least."

"Then you accept?"

"No," said Harold. "It's not enough." Fifty dollars was very enticing. It was just that Harold couldn't see himself carrying the whole thing off. Not for fifty dollars anyway.

"Nonsense," said Boardman almost testily. "It's far above the average fee."

Harold gave a small laugh but did not remind Boardman of his supposed ignorance of such matters. "I'm not an average hustler, though," said Harold. "You're forgetting that I'm a virgin, at least in that way."

"Is that supposed to make you more worthwhile?"

"I thought there was always a higher price on virginity," Harold offered in an objective tone.

Boardman shook his head, as if in wonder. "The degree of veniality you exhibit would seem to indicate exactly the opposite," he said. "You bargain like an experienced hooker."

"Look," said Harold, sitting up with an earnest expression. "This really isn't my thing. I just don't see myself as a hustler, to be honest. But I'm in a bind, financially, and I'd be willing to do it once, if it was really worth my while."

"And what astronomical value do you place upon this unique occasion?" Boardman seemed almost amused.

Harold thought for a moment. "Two hundred dollars," he said. He wasn't sure that was an amount that would make it possible for him to repress his doubts, or one so high as to put Charley-O off altogether. Perhaps it was both.

Boardman laughed. "I almost admire your gall," he said.

Harold shrugged.

"Or is it that you're afraid?"

"What is there to be afraid of?" asked Harold, hoping to be informed.

"Nothing at all," said Boardman. "I'm not a sadist. You wouldn't be required to do anything unnatural."

Harold looked at him, but apparently there was no irony intended.

"I'll offer you one hundred," said Boardman. "I shouldn't, but the circumstances do have their special piquancy. There have been idle moments, as I've watched you grow up, when the thought of one day bedding you has crossed my mind. Although I must say I never expected the situation to actually arise."

"In that case, why did you bother to call me?" asked Harold, suddenly curious.

Boardman smiled. "Well, perhaps you're right. Perhaps it was in the back of my mind. The more proximity one contrives, the higher the percentage of actual conjunction."

"It's a lesson in life," said Harold, quoting from contemporary sources. It occurred to him that he ought to find this conversation far more astonishing than he actually did, but his mother's friends had inured him to the peculiarity of life years ago. Supposedly normal situations had far more capacity to surprise him than did the bizarre.

"One hundred dollars?" said Boardman.

Harold chewed his lip. "I'll think about it," he said.

"Then let's have lunch," said Boardman.

* * *

Harold had sweetbreads for lunch—*ris de veau à la financière*, to be precise. As he devoured these slices of thymus, he contemplated, with less relish, the uses of his own gonads.

He was having a difficult time pinpointing the source of his squeamishness concerning Charley-O's suggestion for post-prandial exercise. One hundred dollars, after all, would give him an additional three weeks in which to solve the problem of continued self-support. Hell, if the experience with Boardman didn't prove too distasteful, it might even provide the solution to the problem in itself.

Somehow, though, Harold was dubious. It was not the morality of selling his body that troubled him. The human body was the most venerable of commercial commodities, and he could at least offer fairly high-class goods. If it had been Mrs. Boardman, would he have hesitated? Undoubtedly not.

Harold speared a slice of olive from his sauce financière. He raised his eyes and perused Boardman's quite handsome face. Charley-O's eyebrows arched in gentle inquiry, and a slight smile touched the corners of his lips. "Do I pass inspection?"

"I'll let you know after I decide on a standard of appraisal," said Harold, irritated at being so transparent.

Harold thought back to the summer of his thirteenth year, during which he had three times joined in a circle jerk in Mulvey's Woods behind his mother's farm. While he had had no subsequent desire to repeat the experience, either on a communal or a more personal basis, he did not recall having found the events in any way traumatic. Quite the contrary, it had all been rather fun, even funny. The situation had had about it the aura of a prank, like throwing stones at streetlights. "A schoolboy prank, the communal wank," Harold thought to himself. It had been an experience divorced from desire, at least so far as he was concerned. Curiosity, certainly, had been present, but none of the desperate need to touch produced in him, only a year or so later, by the sight of a pair of well-developed breasts nestling roundly in a low-cut bodice.

Harold took a sip of Puligny-Montrachet. "Do women's breasts do anything for you?" Harold asked Charley-O.

"Of course, you idiot. Don't be naïve. It's just that I respond to certain masculine attributes as well."

Harold sighed. Perhaps he was missing something. He remembered another Charles, called Chuck, who had been his friend in the groves of academe. Chuck had been queer, or gay, as he preferred to say. Undoubtedly he still was. He had had a letch for Harold, and had told Harold so, once when he was squacked on tequila. Harold had known, anyway, but he was fond of Chuck and it hadn't bothered him to know until Chuck began badgering him about it. The trouble was that when Chuck, his voice slurred with liquor, told Harold how much he wanted to suck his lovely cock, Harold's instrument of that name had blushingly taken it into its head to get hard, all by itself. Harold had tried to hide his hardness, but without success. And Chuck, poor Chuck, could not understand why, if Harold was horny, and Chuck's words had made Harold hard, Harold wouldn't lie back and submit.

Harold had tried to explain that it was exactly because he was fond of Chuck that he wouldn't let him into his pants, that it would seem somehow sad and sick for the head of Chuck, his friend, to be bobbing in his lap.

Chuck had asked, then why are you hard? And Harold had not been able to answer.

Chuck had cried. Chuck had got up and left, suddenly sober. After that he had avoided Harold, on the whole, and when he didn't he looked at Harold out of eyes that seemed not to comprehend, eyes whose strange mixture of accusation and pleading made Harold feel guilty, as though he had betrayed his friend, even when he knew that he had not.

So, while Harold sipped Puligny-Montrachet, speared olives and savored the delicate texture and flavor of sweetbreads, he went over old ground and found no clues. The boy in Mulvey's Woods, he decided, might just as well not have been he, so distant was that experience from his present dilemma. The experiments of adolescence and the choices of manhood, even putative manhood, had nothing in common. For someone else, a boy for whom the experiment in Mulvey's Woods had meant something more than a prank, it might have been different. But for Harold there was no link between that past and this present. And for Boardman he felt no fondness, had no impulse to preserve him from demeaning himself, as he had with Chuck. The present was all new, the past was no guide.

Harold looked at Boardman again. It was not, either, pure physical squeamishness. He did not have to make love to Charley-O after all. There was a slight distaste for the whole situation lurking at the back of his mind, but Harold knew his body well enough to suspect that if he shut off his mind and left it all up to his body, his body would not object to being caressed.

"I don't know," said Harold aloud. "I suppose I'm just scared, really."

One of Harold's better qualities was his ability to be honest, not just with himself but with others, at crucial moments. It almost made up for his habitual flipness.

"What on earth for?" said Charley-O. "I thought we'd been over that."

"I don't know why," said Harold. "Just because it's new, I guess."

"Perhaps you're afraid you'll like it too much," suggested Boardman with a hint of satisfaction.

"That's an unwise remark," Harold said. "If I weren't so busy being honest with myself, it would decide me against you right off."

"Which would only prove that I'm right."

"Which is why I can't allow myself to feel that way." Harold was beginning to feel dizzy, perhaps from the wine.

"Then you agree?" asked Boardman.

Harold realized that he had, in a sense, agreed the moment he had admitted being afraid. "Yes," he said. "To find out why I'm so nervous about it." He took another sip of wine. "And for the money, of course. It's really sort of a good deal, isn't it, a chance to probe my character and get paid for it, too."

"To the logic of youth," said Charley-O, lifting his glass.

*   *   *

Having committed himself, Harold wasn't too sure he could carry it off. What if he couldn't even get a hard-on? Think of the embarrassment.

They took a taxi to Boardman's hotel. As they passed through the narrow streets of the quarter, Harold tried to arouse within himself a spirit of adventure. It would all go much more easily, he thought, if he could manage to persuade himself that he was simply engaged in testing life to its fullest, and put on an attitude at once cynical and—

Harold had been about to say gay. He still felt squeamish.

He told himself, as they swung through the Place St. Sulpice, that an orgasm was an orgasm; hardly a day went by without the achievement of one, usually, in these times of privation, through the tawdry use of his own fist, and how could the fist of another (he attempted to keep his imaginings of the scene on the conservative side) make much difference, why should the thought of it cause such a fluttering of his manly young heart as it pumped through his athletic young body the rich red American blood of a former cub scout?

Harold produced a blush for the doorman as he stepped

out of the taxi in front of the hotel, a small but expensive hostelry favored, according to the Paris *Tribune*, by the American literary establishment. Boardman had a two-room suite. It was decorated in maroon and gold and had a decidedly nineteenth-century air, which pleased Harold in that it made the whole episode seem less real, and more fanciful.

"Take off your jacket," Boardman said, not in any tone of demand but merely politely. "Would you like a cognac?"

"Yes, thank you," said Harold, mustering a reciprocal casualness. He hesitated for a moment, and then removed his sports jacket, laying it across the seat of a straight-backed chair. The room contained another straight-backed chair, but with arms, and a small maroon sofa, one might even have said love seat. Harold considered sitting in the chair, but decided that that would just prolong matters and make them more awkward. It would be best, he assured himself, to consummate this folly as quickly as possible.

Harold crossed to the sofa. He sank back into one corner of it with his legs stretched straight out before him. His genitals, he noted, made a seemly bulge. He really felt as though he were getting into the swing of things. For an instant he was tempted to complete the picture by placing his hands behind his head, with his elbows at a manly angle, but decided that he had gone far enough toward an odalisque posture as it was.

"You look pleased with yourself," said Boardman, handing him a brandy snifter.

"No."

"You're sure you haven't done this before?"

"Yes. Positive." It was galling, Harold felt, how little of his commendable interior nervousness was making itself externally explicit. "What difference would it make if I had?"

"A good deal. The privilege of initiation makes the whole thing considerably more worthwhile. Though whether it's worth a hundred dollars remains to be seen."

"Here's to initiation," said Harold, raising his glass.

"Indeed." Boardman also raised his glass, sipped, and then sat down on the sofa next to Harold, half turning toward him. He ran his hand down Harold's nearest thigh. Harold was wearing summer-weight trousers of a smooth, almost silky synthetic, which served as a conductor for the adagio stroking of Boardman's hand. Harold, however, did his best to feel nothing, focusing his mind upon the budgeting of one hundred dollars over a three-week span.

"You have very muscular thighs," said Boardman. "From swimming?"

"I played hockey at school," said Harold, after a quick review of his athletic career.

"Why don't you relax, Harold?"

"I am relaxed."

"No, you aren't. You aren't allowing yourself any sensual responses."

"Maybe I'm not a very sensual person," said Harold, having a feeble fling at deductive logic.

Boardman ran one finger very slowly up the inside of Harold's thigh and under his balls. In spite of himself, Harold twitched.

"Obviously," said Boardman, "there is no lack of sensual response. It's a matter of keeping your mind busy elsewhere. But that's a hustler's trick. Not the sort of thing one would expect from the uninitiated."

"All right, so I'm sensual. I'm also ticklish," said Harold stoutly. "When I'm excited by somebody, then it's sensuality. At the moment, I'm just ticklish. Like love and hate the two feelings are very close to one another," he concluded.

"You disappoint me, Harold. For a hundred bucks you could at least enjoy yourself a little."

"Are you sure you don't enjoy it more with me being difficult?" Harold asked hopefully.

Boardman laughed. "Try being cooperative and find out." He moved his right hand up over Harold's body, his fingers searching confidently. Through Harold's shirt, Boardman felt his nipples, which, in direct contravention of Harold's command, immediately stiffened.

"That's more like it," said Boardman, with obvious satisfaction. He began to unknot Harold's tie. With the tie off, he undid the first three buttons of Harold's shirt, and his hands moved in against the bare flesh. Harold was not particularly surprised that they should be soft and smooth, but their effect on him was rather more of a shock.

"You have very smooth hands," he said conversationally, in an attempt to keep calm.

"Jergen's Lotion," Boardman replied, leaning forward to lick Harold's neck.

Harold had a very sensitive neck. Still, he was not prepared for the attentive response of his loins. My God, Harold thought, I have the body of a hoor.

Boardman moved upward to Harold's face, attempting to kiss him on the lips. Harold put a hand up and pushed Boardman's head away. "Not on the mouth," he said.

"You make an awful lot of conditions for a bought boy," Boardman said, sitting up.

"I understood bought boys always did that."

"Take off your goddam clothes," said Boardman with sudden anger.

"All right. All right."

Harold stood up and began undoing the rest of the buttons on his shirt, pulling it, as he did so, out of his trousers. He crossed to the chair where he had left his coat.

"Turn so you're facing me," Boardman said. "And take off your shoes and socks next. So many people have the bad aesthetic judgment to take off their socks last."

Harold did as he was told. Oddly enough, the more clothes he removed, the less self-conscious he felt. He was profoundly aware, in one sense, of Boardman's eyes on him, indeed his body responded to that gaze and by the time he was naked he was almost fully erect. Yet he did not feel embarrassed, and his nervousness, his squeamishness, was entirely gone.

Harold laid his shorts on the chair, turned, and raised his eyes to Boardman's.

Boardman smiled. "You're very beautiful," he said.

Harold said nothing. There was nothing to say. When he was small, people had often said to his mother, "What a beautiful little boy you have," and patted Harold on his blond head while his mother smiled and agreed. Harold had concluded rather early in life that it was a nuisance to have people think you were beautiful, and what was more, that it made people treat you like an object a good deal of the time. Besides, he really couldn't see it himself. He knew he was good-looking, in a boyish way, but given a choice he would have preferred to have been built more solidly.

His mother, who was truly beautiful, or at least had been until quite recently, was proud of her beauty, and contemplated it as often as possible. Harold had seen her sit for minutes at a time, perfectly still, moving only her eyes, which sought out, with insatiable curiosity, some seeming secret in the lines and shadows of her mirrored face. Sometimes Harold had the impression, though probably it was only his imagination, that the face in the mirror looked as though it would like to escape the constant gaze of his mother's seeking eyes, as though it were afraid of being found wanting one day.

For himself, Harold avoided mirrors. He shaved looking into a mirror, and combed his hair and tied his tie, but he seldom gave much attention to the contours of the face from which he was removing the morning beard, or to the shape of the head whose hair he was combing. He did his best, in short, to remain innocent of his external appearance. It never occurred to him that this very unconsciousness of his own physical presence only increased his attractiveness to other people, making him more an object of desire, to be sighed over in buses, than many who were basically better looking than himself.

Standing now, naked, on the maroon rug of Boardman's Paris hotel room, Harold was suddenly sharply aware of the expression in the man's eyes, of desire and envy mixed together and intensely focused on his own form. He had seen a covert version of this expression from time to time in the shower rooms of educational and public athletic facilities. He had seen something of it, less covert, but distorted by anguish, in the eyes of Chuck. He had turned away quickly then. In the eyes of the several girls he had slept with he had seen something that he supposed was desire, but not such hungry desire, and the envy replaced by something else, a kind of self-satisfaction, perhaps. It was harder to know what a woman was thinking than a man, which suited Harold just fine. That way you didn't have to acknowledge their admiration as such.

Boardman's expression, however, could not be ignored. It made Harold nervous, not because of anything it revealed about Boardman, but because of what it told him about his own power over Boardman. It wasn't a kind of power Harold had been previously willing to recognize that he possessed. He wasn't at all sure it was a kind of power it made him happy to have.

"I wish you wouldn't look so unhappy," said Boardman.

"I was just thinking."

"What about?"

"The uses of the body," said Harold.

* * *

Harold felt peculiar. His mind and his body were not in agreement. Lying still naked on Charley-O's hotel bed, Harold's body, thoroughly subjugated by Boardman's long experience at giving pleasure, was entirely relaxed. Harold's mind, however, was busy trying to rev up his nerve ends, proselytizing them to join in its disquietude.

The sound of gargling came from the bathroom. It was a sound that depressed Harold. During his second week in Paris, nearly four months earlier, on a gray and violet January day with the mist scudding low above the surface of the Seine, Harold had bought himself the services of a prostitute who was lingering in a doorway on the Boulevard Raspail. She had been reasonably attractive, in her late thirties, perhaps, but owing to the price she was charging and Harold's fear of disease (cowardice and common sense uniting against him once more) he hadn't screwed her. Instead, he had paid half price for a blow job, at the conclusion of which the lady had rushed to the bathroom, spat, and gargled.

Charley-O had swallowed at least, which was a little less conducive to feelings of shame, but there he was gargling away too. The sound was distinctly at odds with the lambency of Harold's limbs, and all too much in tune with the muted cacophony of his busy brain, the more subterranean regions of which were frantically signaling upper levels to abandon their complacency and start feeling guilty. Or were the upper levels signaling the lower? The id, the ego and the superego never seemed willing, in actual practice, to accept the roles so confidently assigned them by dear old Sigmund. Harold contemplated the elaborate corner moldings on the ceiling, and sighed.

Charley-O came out of the bathroom. Harold turned his head to look at him.

"I'll get your clothes," Boardman said, going through to the sitting room with hardly a glance at Harold's recumbent form. It occurred to Harold that Charley-O, too, might be contending with the onslaughts of guilt. A cheering thought, on the whole.

Harold raised himself onto his elbows as Charley-O re-entered the bedroom.

"You can wash up if you like," said Boardman, depositing Harold's clothes, none too neatly, at the bottom of the bed.

His eyes rested briefly on Harold's body. Then he turned away and crossed to the bureau.

Harold got up off the bed and went into the bathroom. There was an efficient-looking modern shower. The term "wash up" did not really suggest the taking of a full-fledged shower, though. Now that it had occurred to him that Boardman was at least as unsettled as he was, Harold began to feel easier about the whole thing. The implied intimacy of taking a shower, which might have bothered him a few minutes before, no longer did. But Charley-O appeared to want to get rid of him as quickly as possible, and Harold certainly had no desire to prolong his stay. He went to the marble sink and washed his genitals and armpits.

These cleansing actions further allayed his inner regrets. Shyly, Harold looked at himself in the shaving mirror. He did not appear to have changed. Toward the end he had groaned a good deal, he recalled. The memory, to his surprise, brought no chagrin. He began to feel almost elated.

As he dried himself, however, Harold suddenly realized that he probably should have brought his clothes with him into the bathroom, or his underwear at least. For an instant he considered wrapping the towel around him before returning to the bedroom. But that seemed sort of ridiculous, given the activities of a few minutes before. He shrugged and walked back into the bedroom naked.

Boardman was standing by the window, looking down at the street. He turned and looked Harold up and down with a distant, almost clinical expression.

"It's too bad women aren't more interested in the male body," he said, in a slightly ironic tone.

Harold stepped into his shorts. "What do you mean?"

"Just what I say. You're obviously proud of your body. But you'll never get it properly appreciated by a woman. Which is too bad, since women are clearly going to get the primary use of it."

Harold buttoned his shirt without looking up, feeling

vaguely insulted. Boardman seemed to be hinting that he'd been less than a satisfactory lay, which Harold found annoying in spite of the passivity of his role.

"I think a lot of women admire men's bodies," Harold said. "Not all of them, I guess, but a lot of them do. Just because they don't say anything doesn't mean they don't notice."

"Aren't we knowledgeable, though," said Boardman with some acidity. "Yes, a few of them do. But not in the way that another man does. Or can."

Buckling his belt, Harold said nothing. He moved to the bureau to tie his tie. Laid out on the top of the bureau was a fifty-dollar bill, together with two twenties and a ten. "I apologize for the American currency," said Boardman. "But it seemed easiest."

"That's fine," said Harold. He pulled the knot of his tie tight and picked up the bills. Crossing back to the bed, he took his wallet out of his jacket and put the money in.

Harold was aware that Charley-O was watching him. As he slipped into his jacket he surprised himself once again by saying, "I'm sorry I was a disappointment." He looked into Boardman's cool gray eyes.

Boardman seemed taken aback. "Don't be silly. It's just that I should know better. When I have sex with young men who are confirmed homosexuals, I usually have a very happy time, if they're any good in bed at all. Afterward I feel entirely at peace with myself. With a professional hustler, it's more chancy. But young men who are basically straight, like yourself, simply make me sad. I don't know why. But I should know better by now."

Harold could think of nothing to say. "I'm sorry," he repeated stupidly.

Boardman shook his head.

"I think perhaps, though, I will tell your father that I was unable to reach you, if you don't mind. It seems simpler. Unless you have some special message, of course."

"No," said Harold.

Boardman moved toward him and extended his hand. "Goodbye, Harold." His grip was lawyerly, firm but impersonal.

"Goodbye," said Harold. "Thank you for lunch." The inanity of this remark was apparent to Harold at once, but Boardman did not smile. "You're very welcome," he said.

Harold felt as though he ought to say something more. For a moment, it was like being with Chuck again. It was as though he had failed Boardman, somehow, by being himself instead of fulfilling Boardman's fantasy. Harold's experience had never convinced him that you could be true to yourself without falsifying other people's expectations of you. Polonius clearly had his head wedged.

There really wasn't anything else to be said to Boardman, Harold decided, and so he left. He had three weeks in his pocket, and he went back out into the City of Light.

4 / War

"H ARRROLD!"

From some distance away, over the hill behind him, a voice was calling. Sam's voice. The sound dwindled quickly in the afternoon heat. It was too far away for Harold to be bothered to acknowledge it, and he didn't want company anyway.

In a field a half mile below his mother's country house, basking nude on a blanket in the August sun, Harold contemplated the shimmer in the air above the long grass separating the edge of the mown field from the woods beyond; gradually he lifted his eyes to the tops of those dense woodland trees where, in sharp relief against the high blue sky, the green leaves stirred in a westerly breeze.

"A tunnel of green gloom," whispered Harold to himself. He had read Rupert Brooke when he was fourteen, an impressionable age.

Harold heard his name float once again over the hot countryside, but from still farther away.

He looked up at the sky and didn't answer. To the perfection of the day he had attributed a symbolic significance, taking it as an outward manifestation of his inner satisfaction. Everything seemed to be going his way, thanks to a run of sheer good luck that had begun in Paris one bright May day as beautiful as this August one, when he had been on his way to meet an American girl in the Luxembourg Gardens. Pam, rosy-cheeked and strawberry blond, a cliché of loveliness on the rebound from a French philanderer, had climbed into bed with the first boy from back home she could find, and that boy happened to be Harold. Pam had also, to help Harold financially and at the same time make clear her superiority (or so Harold surmised), hired him to take a couple of reels of eight-millimeter film of her as she wandered about Paris, posing in front of landmarks and looking virginal for the benefit of her Daddy back in Detroit.

Harold had therefore had a new film in his camera that May morning, and so was able to use the entire footage when the front blew out of a small hotel on the rue Dauphine just as he turned into the block. Two people had been killed, several injured, and an English honeymoon couple had discovered themselves making whoopee for the world at large. Harold had got all of it, including the honeymooners, although their graphic demonstration of the trauma that can ensue from *coitus interruptus* was sadly edited out of the versions seen by the general public.

Terrorist violence (the hotel turned out to be owned by the father of a colonel in an Algerian-based paratroop unit), falling masonry, gore on the sidewalks, weeping women and hysterical lovers from abroad—it was all there, a sensational piece of reportage. As soon as the reel had been run through, Harold dashed for a phone and called a young American television producer named Mike Whaley, who was in Paris to get some local footage for a documentary on the Algerian situation. Mike had done an interview with Harold's stepfather two years earlier, as part of an educational film on new directions in art (sideways, Sam had suggested). Only two days before the explosion at the hotel,

Harold had recognized Mike sitting at the Deux Magots and reintroduced himself.

With Mike Harold worked out a deal that allowed him to collect not only on the film but on a number of stills from it, two of which he sold to *Paris Match*. All together, Harold had managed to make almost three thousand dollars out of his bit of luck, money that had made it possible for him to return to the States without asking his parents for help or acceding to their conditions. What was more, Mike Whaley had promised Harold he'd help him get a job in television in New York.

The sound of cicadas rose from the edge of the woods, like the noise of heat itself. Harold stretched luxuriously, in full contentment. He'd been back in the States for two weeks, mostly spent at his mother's. Mike Whaley was on location in India, working on another project, and Harold was merely killing time until Labor Day. After more than a year in Europe, a period of reacclimation had seemed like a good idea.

"Harold! For Christ's sake."

Sam's voice came again, suddenly much closer and clearly annoyed.

Harold sighed. "Yes," he called back.

Sam came out of the woods on the slope above the field. Dressed in his usual attire of jeans and a Viyella shirt (of which he had more than twenty, mostly courtesy of Harold's mother), he sauntered down toward Harold, taking his time. Sam always took his time.

Harold turned over on his stomach and watched him approach.

"Hello, Sam."

"Hello, bareass. How's your asthma?"

"What asthma?"

"Never had asthma?"

"Nope. So what?"

"Your Uncle Sam has his eye on you, that's what."

"Getting formal in your old age, aren't you?"

"Not me, kid. THE Uncle Sam."

Harold's stomach lurched beneath him. "What are you talking about? Not the draft?"

"You're going to go a long way, Hal baby, with smarts like that," said Sam. "Your Dad called from New York. Seems the army wants to give you a pre-induction physical."

"How soon?"

"You've got a couple of weeks."

"Great. That's really wonderful." Harold put his head down in his arms for a moment. "Just when things start working right for me."

"Yeah, I know, it's a tough break." Sam squatted down, plucking a blade of grass to chew on. "It was bound to come, though, kid. Better now than after you got settled into a job."

"Like hell. That kind of job you get through connections. If I'd worked for a while then I'd have some credits to get me started again later."

"Well, my friend, that's life for you. Look at it this way, what would civilization be without war, boredom, death and stupidity? You need them to make the rest of it seem precious, right? And there's nothing like the military for offering you contrasts with the better things in life."

"I'll take my chances on losing perspective," said Harold with a lightness he didn't feel. It was hard to say what in fact he did feel. Numb. The sun burned down on his back. He could hear the cicadas sawing away as determinedly as ever. It was hard to believe that things could change so fast, and yet his run of good luck had been just as sudden.

"It's enough to shake your belief in the pathetic fallacy," said Harold.

"How's that?" said Sam. Sam was much admired as an artist, but he hadn't read a book in twenty years.

"A literary term," said Harold. "I thought this weather was all for me. It fit my mood so perfectly."

"Oh, that bit. Yeah, well, if it'll make you feel any better, we're supposed to have a thunderstorm before dark."

"You're full of reassuring words, aren't you, Sam?"

Sam chuckled. "I do my best."

"Did Dad want me to call?"

"I don't know. Your mother talked to him. Maybe you'd better get the facts from your father."

Harold laughed at this reference to his mother's inability to keep things straight. But Sam, chomping on a new blade of grass, refused this time to acknowledge his own humor.

"I'll call him later," said Harold. "I want to think things over first."

Sam took the grass out of his mouth. "You going to try and beat it?"

Harold shrugged. The sweat was gathering in the small of his back. "I don't know. Maybe." He looked up at Sam in hope of guidance.

"I wouldn't blame you for it, kid. When I was fighting the Krauts the word was that we were saving civilization. I guess I believed that, but I still wasn't sure it was worth it."

Having delivered himself of this uncharacteristic piece of self-revelation, Sam stood up. "It's your decision, though," he said. "I'd hate to be accused of corrupting my stepson as well as the world of art."

"That's all right, Sam," said Harold. "We trust and admire you, even so."

"Thanks, kid. In this world, a man needs all the friends he can get."

*   *   *

Harold, although strong on natural common sense, was less apt at formal philosophic debate, especially when he had had no previous reason to give a subject his committed attention. Great moral decisions, it had occurred to him, could by definition be made only under stress.

Now under stress, Harold realized that he had never

given much thought to the subject of war and peace. It was just not something that thrilled him. Even novels on the subject left him cold; he had failed to finish not only Tolstoy's lofty amplification of the theme but Norman Mailer's dissection of its entrails. Films interested him rather more, simply because of his fascination with the medium. But the best of such films, *Paths of Glory* or *Forbidden Games*, always seemed to take a negative viewpoint. Portraits of bravery never seemed to work on the screen, at least for Harold, because they could never avoid the glorification of death. Bravery, now that Harold turned his attention to the subject, was obviously most effectively presented in verse, where the fine words could not be undercut by visual images of torn and bleeding flesh.

Harold had to admit it—he was quite simply prejudiced against war. There were numerous arguments to counter this prejudice, he noted in the course of a thorough perusal of *Bartlett's*. Machiavelli held that a prince should have no other aim nor thought, nor study anything else but the organization and discipline of war. But then, Harold was not a prince, except perhaps to some of his female acquaintances (and although the term had been applied to him after one or another splendidly thoughtful act like buying a bunch of violets, he doubted its serious intent). Also, Machiavelli was made to look decidedly shabby in the light of a copycat statement written for the Italian Encyclopedia by a man named Mussolini, to the effect that war alone brought to its highest tension all human energy and put the stamp of nobility upon those peoples with the courage to face it.

Harold was simply not persuaded by such braggadocio. And other famous figures were entirely less sanguine on the subject. Harold was relieved to discover, for instance, that Benjamin Franklin had given out the opinion that there never was a good war nor a bad peace. Harold made a mental note to throw that in the face of his draft board if necessary. Nothing, he had discovered, was more disconcerting to the Legionnaire type than to be confronted by the left-wing statements of the founders of their country, gentlemen who, being revolutionaries, had a goodly number of anti-establishment remarks to their credit.

Sophocles, Harold was unsurprised to find, was among the most pessimistic commentators on the theme, even going so far as to write that war never slew a bad man in its course, but the good always. Much as Harold would have liked to go along with that, he thought probably Anacreon was nearer the mark when he suggested that war spared not the brave but the cowardly. On the other hand, Sophocles also wrote that war loved to prey upon the young, which was clearly an eternal verity. So much so, in fact, that even Herbert Hoover had been led to announce that, "Older men declare war. But it is the young that must fight and die."

"Herbert Hoover," exclaimed Harold aloud, and decided on the spot that he need goggle no longer at the words of the great. His mind was made up.

*   *   *

"Darling, I'm so sorry."

Harold was wearing only shorts; he steeled himself for his mother's embrace, knowing that her hands would, as always, be cold.

"Maybe I can get out of it," he said.

"Do you think so?"

"I'm going to try."

His mother gave a sigh and shook her bracelets. "It's too bad you're not queer," she said. "I mean, I wouldn't want you to be queer, darling, but it would be convenient just now, wouldn't it?"

"Yes, Mother, it would. That's a possibility. I might be able to persuade them that I am."

"Good heavens, but how?" She reached nervously for a cigarette, her hands fluttering. "I mean, you aren't, are you? They always say Mother is the last to know."

Harold had to smile. "No, I'm not queer, Mother. To the despair of some of your friends."

"Which friends? Oh, never mind, it doesn't matter. I'm really a terrible parent, aren't I?" She held up a hand and waved it dismissively. "Don't answer that, darling, it's not a good question."

Harold sometimes had the feeling that hiding somewhere inside his mother's baroque personality was a plain colonial one, afraid to come out. Yet, if she were going to show it to anyone, you would have thought it would be to her only child, and she treated him just as she did everyone else.

"The thing that worries me, though," she said, "about saying you're queer if you're not, is that they might find out and make things all the worse for you. I mean, they might send you to Siberia, or something."

"That's in Russia, Mother."

"Yes, yes, of course, but I mean its democratic equivalent. You musn't take me so literally, Harold. You've been doing it a lot since you came back. I'm sorry, I know it must be a bore always having to translate me, as it were. If only I could think as fast as I talk. I mean, the outline is there, but my mind just doesn't fill in the details as fast as it should. Thank heavens you have your father's brain. Though you don't have his personality, which is also to the good. So stuffy. I hope you won't ever become stuffy, my love."

"I hope I won't either, Mother." It occurred to Harold, however, that the impatience (verging on embarrassment) he often felt in connection with his mother was close to being a kind of stuffiness. And that was foolish, he ought simply to be amused, like Sam was in his dry way.

"Are there any other ways of getting out of it, dear? I'll do anything I can to help."

"Well, there are lots of physical defects—asthma, trick knees, a heart murmur, ulcers, that kind of thing, but I doubt if I can find anything seriously enough wrong with me in the physical line. So it's got to be something psychological. I guess the best idea would be to talk to a psychiatrist, if I can find a sympathetic one."

"Oh, well, that's easy, darling. I know lots of psychiatrists. Should it be one I've been to myself, or just a friend?"

Harold was quite certain that if it was one his mother had been to, the man could hardly help but be prepared to meet a maladjusted son. "That's hard to know," said Harold, tactfully.

"I have just the man," said his mother, stabbing the air with her cigarette. "Of course your father abhors him, but that doesn't really matter, does it? He's not going to like the whole idea, is he?"

"I'm sure he won't," said Harold. "Who's the man?"

"His name is Braden Phillips. He's an old beau of mine, I grew up with him, actually." There was a sudden light in her eye as she glanced at Harold. "Your father never did like the idea of anyone having known me longer than he had. I wonder if he's as jealous of that mere child he's seeing so much of these days? Maggie. Maggie—"

"Mason," said Harold, with as much detachment as possible. "Will you call Dr. Phillips for me?"

"Of course, darling. I'll do it right now." She took one of his hands and patted it. "I don't want you to be a soldier," she said. "It's strange, you'd think I'd like the uniforms, so many women do. But I never have, even as a girl. Not even sailors."

"Don't say too much to Dr. Phillips, though, Mother. Just that I've received a draft notice and would like to talk to him. It's better to play it by ear."

"Yes, of course. That's the trouble with your father, he thinks you can control life, make up a set of rules and follow them. But that's impossible, isn't it, love? You must always be ready to improvise. Improvise, improvise," said his mother.

*   *   *

The train moved slowly through the Connecticut countryside, down from the lake region to Hartford and New Haven, stopping every ten minutes at one small pseudo-gothic outhouse of a station after another to take on ladies in white gloves and flowered hats (that looked in need of watering) or baggy-suited businessmen, the grayness of whose faces was only partially masked by weekend tans and the flush of alcohol; a string of dusty cars with stained windows and broken seats creeping hesitantly toward New York, carrying the women to end-of-summer sales and the men to whatever toil would make it possible for them to send the ladies forth again next month to purchase brown suede gloves and hats with autumn berries on them—an inexorable round trip through the years, as grindingly slow, as joyless, as full of frustration as the passage of the train itself through the stifling August heat toward the eventual bowels of Manhattan.

Harold was in a really stinking mood.

For one thing, he missed his Ferrari more than at any time since he'd sold it when he went to Europe over a year and a half ago. At moments like this, when the world seemed entirely against you, there was nothing quite so re-assuring, in Harold's view, as to be behind the wheel of a car that was your own and preferably a Ferrari. It fostered a feeling of control, an illusion that you were the master of your fate. The only trouble was, of course, that so many human beings found this illusion enthralling, even the ordi-nary illusion to be gained with a Chevrolet, that the auto-mobile was beginning to defeat its own psychological ends, to say nothing of its practical ones. Each additional car on the road, each additional participant in the derby, brought a lessening of the promised exhilaration. It made Ferraris more to be coveted than ever, Harold was aware, since only a greater and greater potential for speed and performance could compensate for the lack of open road on which to use it.

Depressed by this paradox, Harold sighed and looked out

the window, through the bird shit. They were approaching
New Haven and the air was turning yellow. If it was New
Haven that the forces of freedom were massed to protect,
Harold was damned if he'd lift a finger to help. His father
had wanted him to go to Yale, in fact, but it had taken
Harold only ten minutes in that gray, decrepit city and one
glance at the gloomy, turreted towers of Yale itself to set
him against his father's wishes. Some day, Harold was sure,
he would find something in which his own desire echoed his
father's, allowing him one blinding moment of filial epiph-
any, but Yale had not provided the spark.

The train churned to a stop in the New Haven station. On
the platform just outside Harold's window, a soldier waited
to board the train. His duffle bag beside him, he stood impassively, the sweat dripping from his face and dark patches
showing under his arms. He was quite small; his pale skin
was set off by dark hair and high cheekbones, making him
look very young and fragile. Harold had a momentary lapse
of his cowardice; if someone as vulnerable looking as that
could take it, then Harold, who was at least physically
strong, surely ought to be able to survive. He put the
thought aside. It wasn't going to help things to start getting
manly on himself.

A few moments later the soldier approached down the
aisle of the car. There was an empty seat beside Harold; the
only other free ones were beside women. The soldier
stopped and asked if the seat was taken.

Harold shook his head. "Help yourself."

The soldier heaved his duffle bag up onto the rack and
collapsed into the seat. "Christ, what heat," he said, and
closed his eyes.

Half an hour later he stirred and sat up. "I thought these
cars were supposed to be air-conditioned," he said.

"Supposed to be is right," said Harold, rousing himself out
of his funk.

"Well, it's too hot to sleep. You got anything to read?"

"Sure," said Harold, handing over the copy of *Playboy* the soldier had been eyeing. "How long've you been in?"

"Nineteen months," the soldier replied, flipping pages. "Only five to go. Four months and twenty-two days, in fact."

"I can tell you really like it a lot," said Harold.

The soldier gave a short, grunting laugh. "Being in the army is like spending two years on a train." He passed his fingers lightly across the plastic-looking flesh of the Play-mate of the Month. "Fucking airbrushes," he said.

*   *   *

Harold was sitting in the living room drinking a gin and tonic when his father arrived home from his office.

"Hello, Harold. I see you've made yourself at home."

"I thought it was my home," said Harold, who was in no mood to take any moralistic crap. "One of them, anyway."

Almost imperceptibly, his father winced. "Indeed. I just don't approve of drinking in the afternoon. It is one of your mother's more unfortunate habits."

"Mother does it because she's bored. I'm doing it because I'm hot and under stress," said Harold implacably. "But I'll stop at six, if it'll make you feel better."

His father pretended he was not amused. "It's really none of my business. You're your own man now, as you so often remind me."

Harold looked at the floor.

After a brief pause, his father said, "At any rate, you're right about the heat. I believe I'll have a drink myself."

Although he knew that, following such an admission, his father would be smiling at him, Harold declined to raise his eyes to acknowledge this token of affection. Harold and his father were expert at playing ships-that-pass-in-the-night, and even though their mutual determination never to be bested by the other often made Harold tired and even sad, whenever the chance came for him to break the circle, he refused to take it. But then, his father never took such op-portunities when they were offered by Harold. It was a virtual standoff. Harold suspected that there were moments when his father too would have liked to change things between them, but those moments never seemed to come to them simultaneously.

His father remained standing in front of him, his highly polished loafers gleaming in the light from the lamp on the table behind the sofa. He seldom wore tie shoes unless it was absolutely necessary; it was a curiously informal characteristic of an otherwise rather formal man.

Turning away, his father crossed to the teak bar in the corner. Harold's mother, who collected French furniture, had always insisted that the bar be relegated to the study. One of the first things Harold's father had done after the divorce was to move it into the living room. "I don't blame you for feeling low, Harold," he said, putting ice into a glass. "Nobody likes to have his plans turned upside down. But I think you'll find that if you try to make the best of things, even the army can offer some rewarding experiences."

"Would you care to name three?" asked Harold.

His father paused in the act of pouring gin and looked around. "You might well be able to get into the photographic corps, for one possibility. You are interested in photography, I believe. Or do you know everything about the subject already?"

"No, of course not. But I could learn even more working in television, and at the same time be free to lead my own life."

"That may be, Harold. But, facing facts, since you're going to have to serve in the army, I simply wish to point out that it needn't be a total loss."

"I'm not going to serve in the army, Dad, under any circumstances," Harold said quietly.

His father picked up his drink and crossed back to the high-backed armchair next to the sofa where Harold was slumped. "And how do you plan to avoid it?"

"I'm not sure. Any way I can."

His father wrinkled his nose, as though in subconscious anticipation of a bad smell. "Any way?"

"I'm not going to serve. Period. For starters, I'm going to see Braden Phillips tomorrow afternoon."

"Good God. Your mother's pals. One is never rid of them."

"Mother said you disliked him."

"I do, but that's beside the point. What do you expect him to do for you?"

"Hopefully, he'll be willing to attest that I'm not psychologically fit to serve."

"Oh, come off it, Harold. You've used that kind of argument before. That summer you didn't want to work at the yacht club you came up with the same line."

"I was being facetious then, Dad."

"Were you indeed? And now you're not?" His father stretched his legs before him, ankles crossed, loafers gleaming.

"No. I'm not psychologically suited to the army. In fact, I think most people are unsuited to it, and those who do fit right in are dangerous and destructive. They all ought to be sent off to fight little wars in Antarctica or someplace with all the natural soldiers from everywhere else, while the rest of us live in peace."

"Please spare me the undergraduate idealism, Harold. What you say may have a grain of truth in it somewhere, but it is totally without realistic application."

"It wouldn't be, if enough people went along with it."

"That's perfect drivel. I really have no patience with this sort of foolishness. It's time you grew up, Harold. You're not talking about the real world."

"Exactly."

"I beg your pardon?" His father's blue eyes were professionally condescending.

"You've just granted me my case. I'm not in touch with reality. Quite clearly, I won't be able to function properly in the army."

"I don't think mere sophistry is going to do the trick for you, Harold."

"Oh, I plan to dress it up some. Roll my eyes, twitch a little."

His father met this sally with silence. After a pause of sufficient length to convey the depth of his contempt, he said, "Of course you realize that if you don't go, someone else will be called up in your place."

"Not quite, Dad. They'll be asked to go, I grant you, but that's not to say they will go."

"You'd ask them, then, to be as irresponsible as you are, and refuse in turn?"

"That's not the way I see it. The thing is that nobody is going to resist unless he's got his back against the wall. If I can beat the system, then somebody else will be called up and will have to make a decision. If he hasn't got the courage, or common sense, or appropriate cowardice, to refuse to serve, and to use any and all means to avoid serving, then that's his failure, not mine."

His father stared at him. "I really don't understand why you didn't want to go into the law, Harold. Your ability to argue a spurious point into the ground is nothing short of staggering."

"Are you complimenting me or running down the law?"

His father did not appear amused. "My son the gadfly," he said, in a tone that mingled derision with resignation.

"There are worse things to be," said Harold.

"Indeed. My son the draft dodger. It fills the parental heart with pride, Harold, I can tell you."

Harold bit his lip. He felt very tired. "I'm sorry, Dad," he said.

"Are you really? And what for?"

"I seem to do nothing but disappoint you."

"Oh, don't apologize. It clearly gives you considerable satisfaction to disappoint. I find that distressing, but I don't see that I can hold you entirely responsible. I know perfectly well that I have disappointed you, too. And now, if you'll excuse me, I must shower and change. I have a dinner engagement."

"Who with?" asked Harold, although he knew the answer.

His father gave him a sharp look, as though to indicate it was none of Harold's business. But then he said, "With Maggie Mason."

"Are you going to marry her?" Harold asked. He himself didn't care one way or the other, but for some reason his mother was anxious to find out.

His father rubbed the heel of his hand against his temple, looking suddenly weary. "I don't know, Harold. She's still quite a young woman, and she wants to have children. I'm afraid I don't."

Harold swallowed. "Oh, you may yet live not to regret me, Dad. Don't give up so easily."

Harold had surprised himself with this remark, and it appeared that he had also managed to startle his father, who stared at him for a moment as though trying to remember where they had met before. Then something that was almost a smile passed across his face. "You do have spirit, Harold, I will say that for you. What I meant to indicate, however, was simply that fatherhood doesn't interest me, and brings me no particular joy. That's my fault, although I'm afraid it has been your problem. I don't approve of what you're doing with your life, Harold. It has no plan, you seem to make up the rules as you go along. When you get bored with college, or decide you don't want to serve in the army, you come up with some instant philosophy that will permit you to move in the direction you want at the given moment. It lacks consistency and to me it seems merely irresponsible. And please don't quote Emerson at me, as you did once a few years ago. It was *foolish* consistency he was speaking about; I don't believe he intended to throw the baby out with the bath."

"But everything's inconsistent today, Dad. Half the time when I have to make a choice about something, I just want to say, 'None of the above.' The only thing that makes any sense is to play it by ear. So, that's what I'm doing."

"I'm sure, Harold, that you do honestly feel that way. But I don't understand why. It simply confuses me. All I can do is tell you what I think is right. If you disagree, then you must do what you think is right—and accept the consequences."

His father was standing so that his face was illuminated only by the light from the window beside him; the sky had clouded over and the late afternoon light had taken on a curiously flat violet tinge that turned his father's face quite gray.

"I'll accept the consequences," said Harold.

*   *   *

"Well now, Harold," said Dr. Phillips, "your mother tells me you have a problem with the draft."

"Yes, that's right," said Harold.

"Not an uncommon complaint, of course." The doctor's almost too handsome face looked as though it had been given a surgical lift.

"I suppose it isn't," said Harold.

"Of course there's no question that a negative attitude toward the military can lead to an unhappy time in the service. But I expect we can find a way to help you out."

"I hope so," said Harold.

"After all, the most important function of psychiatry is to help people in the development of positive attitudes."

"I beg your pardon," said Harold.

"Most psychological problems are caused by negative attitudes of one sort or another, Harold. When the reasons for those attitudes are uncovered, and the negativism can be shown to be based upon false assumptions, then a more positive, healthier outlook can be built upon revised assumptions."

"I think my mother must have confused things, doctor," Harold said with a sinking feeling.

Dr. Phillips lifted his chiseled chin and stared at Harold. "Really?" he said after a pause. "And do you often feel that your mother is confusing the issue?"

Harold began to wonder how well Dr. Phillips and his mother actually knew one another. "Most of the time, yes."

"I see. Do you feel that she is deliberately misrepresenting you, or that it is a result of natural error?"

"Oh, it's certainly not deliberate. She just doesn't stop to think what she's saying." Although, in fact, Harold sometimes wondered.

"You feel then that you are only an inadvertent victim?"

"I don't feel like a victim at all," said Harold.

"No? And yet you claim that your mother habitually misrepresents you, that she has in fact misrepresented you to me."

"Yes, but—"

"Let's just clarify one thing at a time, please, Harold."

"That's what I'm trying to do, just clarify one thing. Maybe my mother didn't misrepresent me at all. Maybe you misunderstood her."

"Really? And why should I do a thing like that?"

Harold felt as though he were walking on a treadmill. "Look, Dr. Phillips, the point is that I don't want to develop a positive attitude toward the army. I want you to certify that my attitude is in fact so negative that I would be more trouble than I'm worth."

Dr. Phillips pursed his lips in a disapproving grimace. "I see," he said. "I see. You wish to retain your negativism, then?"

"Exactly."

The doctor shook his head and selected a pipe out of the rack beside his desk. "But you see, Harold," he said, "my job is to cure people of their problems, not to sanctify them. Perhaps you should see a priest. If your feelings about the army were couched in the terms of conscientious objection, that would be positivistic, you would be taking a moral stand. Moral stands, being positivistic, are to be admired. But if I were to certify your negativism, then I would be condoning it. And that would be a negative action on my part. That's the trouble with negativism, you see, it's so terribly catching, one is constantly exposed to its dangers. I'm sorry, Harold, but I can't do it. It goes against the grain, that's all."

Dr. Phillips, who had been filling his pipe as he talked, now proceeded to light it. Like all pipe smokers, he pretended to be unaware of the theatricality of his habit.

"But my situation is not entirely governed by negativism, doctor," said Harold loudly, trying to compete with the pipe for Dr. Phillips' attention. "I am, in fact, taking a positive moral stand. A stand against war. If there were no armies, no wars could be fought, right? By resisting the draft I am resisting war. Surely you don't think war is a positive force?" Borrowing a sheaf from his mother's script, Harold was talking faster than he was thinking, and hoping for the best.

"Well, now." Dr. Phillips made balancing motions with his hands. "It does of course have its destructive aspects. But it also provides an outlet for impulses that might otherwise lead to revolution. A war against external forces is much to be preferred to internal revolution. Revolution is negativism at its most rampant. Positively cancerous," said Dr. Phillips, drawing on his pipe with a self-righteous, liquid sound.

"I would have thought it was the other way around," Harold suggested gingerly. "It seems to me that those who maintain the status quo are looking backward, and are therefore negativists, while those who press for revolution are looking forward and are therefore positivists."

Dr. Phillips looked momentarily perplexed. His eyes crossed slightly as he contemplated the bowl of his pipe. Then he appeared to see his way forward: his eyes closed and opened again and met Harold's straight on. "You are talking about social forces, I believe, Harold, whereas I am speaking of personal motivation. Revolutionaries may be good for society, in the long run, but they're hell on themselves and their families—seldom very stable, you understand."

"Are you saying that war is good?" asked Harold, attempting to get a few things pinned down, if not clarified.

Phillips took his pipe out of his mouth. "My dear young man, you know perfectly well that's not what I meant."

"Then it must be evil." Harold was determined to close all hatches.

Dr. Phillips' eyes retreated warily. "In the ideal state," he granted, "there would be no war. But to achieve an ideal state, it will first be necessary to perfect the workings of the human mind, to eradicate all traces of negativism."

"Fine," said Harold. "So you can see that by refusing to serve in the military forces that make war possible, I am taking a positive step, even though a small one, toward the eventual achievement of Utopia. It seems to me, doctor, that I deserve your help in such an endeavor."

Dr. Phillips grunted. "Have you consulted your family physician?" he queried.

"I have no physical defects that would keep me from serving," said Harold. "And since my religious upbringing was lax, to say the least, I have no affiliation with any church that could serve to back up a plea as a conscientious objector. The army's very tough on that subject, I hear. So I've got to find another way to deal with the situation. The most effective would be your testament as to my psychological incompatibility with army life."

"Now Harold," said Dr. Phillips, "in what ways exactly are you incompatible with army life?"

"I refuse to be told what to do."

"You mean that you don't like to be told what to do. But that's common to us all to a greater or lesser degree."

"It is?" said Harold, allowing himself to be sidetracked once again. "I know people who go to pieces if they aren't told what to do."

"You let me worry about the masochists," said Dr. Phillips. "They are not blessed with normal responses. The sadist, in comparison with the masochist, is a very healthy type. Masochists are so—"

"Negative," said Harold.

"You said it," said Dr. Phillips.

"Look, Dr. Phillips, it's not merely that I don't like to take orders. I refuse to take orders."

"Does that mean that you refuse to stop when there's a red light? Or that you'll refuse to pay your income tax once you've begun to earn your own living?"

"I'm already earning my own living," said Harold. "But those rules are ones that everybody has to obey. People are always managing to avoid the draft, though, because of where they live or their profession or their height, you name it. And I'm not going to be one of the ones to go when so many do not go. I simply refuse." Harold decided to stop before his high moral tone slipped any further.

"Well, we'll have to see about that, won't we? Let's assume, just for the moment, that you are in the army. What is your reply going to be when the sadistic sergeant takes away your weekend pass because he found you reading *Tropic of Cancer*? Hmmm? Are you really going to make things worse for yourself, get yourself thrown in the brig by arguing with him and refusing to get rid of Mr. Miller's dirty book? Hmmm? Well?"

"That's a well-chosen example," said Harold, acknowledging his passion for culture. "I guess I'd just have to kill him."

"Oh, come now, Harold."

"Kill, kill, kill," yelled Harold at the top of his voice, leaping to his feet and banging on the doctor's desk.

Dr. Phillips steadfastly sucked on his pipe. "Sit down, Harold," he said. "Emotional outbursts are bad for the blood pressure."

The intercom buzzed, and the doctor flicked it on. "Are you all right, doctor?" Harold could hear a quaver in the secretary's voice and was glad he had frightened somebody aside from himself. He felt dizzy and his heart was pounding vehemently.

"Yes, yes, everything's fine, Miss Spivak, don't worry about it—just a small case of retrogression."

Dr. Phillips leaned back in his chair. "If only we could channel that blood lust properly, Harold, we could make a fine soldier out of you. You might even want to make it a career. Such deep feelings of antagonism, appropriately directed, are essential to the makeup of the professional soldier. Or policeman, for that matter."

"I'm only antagonistic when I'm pushed around," said Harold sullenly. "I just want to be left alone."

"Yes, that presents a problem," said Dr. Phillips. "The military man must wish to kill at all times. I'm told the armed forces are rife with psychological problems just now, among the career officers. There hasn't been anything that could really be called a war in ten years, since Ike went to Korea. That's very demoralizing to a career officer, you know. It irks them even more that this long lull was brought on by the promises of a former general, just so he could get into the White House. After all, your career officer has put in years learning how to destroy, and here he is all het up with nobody to practice on. And there are so few promotions when things are peaceful. It's not a happy situation for them. Very negative. I'll bet the Pentagon is just combing the intelligence reports for a good war situation. They'll have to come up with something pretty solid, though, Kennedy's not going to bite at just any bait after that bad experience with the Bay of Pigs. I've heard rumors, however, that Cardinal Spellman is very concerned about his Catholic brethren in Vietnam. He thinks we should intervene. Now there's a powerful voice in terms of the current situation. On the other hand, when the military has got to depend on prelates to manufacture their wars for them, things are in a bad way. That kind of stuff went out in the Middle Ages."

"I couldn't agree with you more," said Harold. "But if we're going to have another war some place, that's just one more reason to stay out of the army. I'm certainly not going to fight Cardinal Spellman's crusades for him. From what I hear, he's just looking for another place to tour the front, so he can go down on his knees for the good of the boys, as they say. That's certainly having your wafer and eating it too, isn't it? Anyway, I'm not going into the army, and if you won't help me, then I have only one alternative left."

"What's that?"

"I'll have to say I'm queer."

"Harold, why didn't you say so in the first place? I never would have guessed. You certainly don't look queer. But then fewer and fewer of them do these days. At any rate, that's all you had to tell me. We needn't have spent all this time discussing moral stands. You really didn't have to be afraid to talk about it, you know. I've treated many homosexuals, and been very successful on the whole. Forty percent have eventually married and had children. I wouldn't swear that some of them don't occasionally get up to no good in subway men's rooms and turkish baths, but nobody's perfect. If you'd like to try to work your problem out with me, Harold, I'd be glad to help. I must insist, however, that you genuinely desire to change. It's no good trying, otherwise."

"But, doctor, I'm not homosexual," said Harold, torn between discretion and the better part of valor.

"Now, look, Harold, I'm not censuring you. I realize the kind of guilt feelings a young man can develop in this situation, but it's foolish to try to keep the facts from me. I'll prepare a letter stating that you're psychologically unfit to serve, and do it without hesitation now that I know that is in fact the case. The army doesn't want homosexuals, especially those orally inclined—they're more corrupting, it's felt. Or do you like to be buggered? Never mind, you don't have to tell me, unless you decide you want to become a regular patient. In fact, there's no need for me to say anything too specific in my letter. I can quite understand that if you should manage to achieve a heterosexual adjustment in the years to come you wouldn't want to have it in your army record that you're a sexual deviant. So we'll just be a bit vague."

"Thank you," said Harold, abandoning valor.

"I'm sorry you couldn't have confided in me at the start, Harold, it would have saved a lot of time. But it was good to talk with you and get to know you a bit." Dr. Phillips got up and came around from behind his desk with his hand extended. Harold stood and shook hands. "I was very fond of your mother, you know. Of course, I won't say anything to her about our discussion here."

All Harold could manage was a nod. He appeared to be free of the army, but he hardly felt that he had regained any control over his own destiny. Feeling dazed, he started for the door. Dr. Phillips put a hand on his shoulder. "One little piece of advice, Harold. If you should decide to try yourself with a woman one of these days, don't make it a prostitute. That will only confirm your distaste. Look for a nice girl your own age who's had a little experience. A virgin's not the best idea, either, when you're squeamish. Breaking that cherry can be a pretty messy experience. But do give it a try some time or other. You might surprise yourself."

"I suppose anything's possible," said Harold.

5 / Filth

HAROLD became obsessed by sex.

"Harold, you're becoming obsessed," said Spike, who had been Harold's roommate at school, gone to college on the West Coast and recently returned to New York.

"It's because I'm bored," said Harold. "My mother drinks because she's bored. I fuck because I'm bored."

"You mean if you weren't bored you wouldn't fuck? You're kidding yourself, my friend."

"Well, if the rest of my life were more interesting, I wouldn't fuck so much," Harold said. "I wouldn't have time, would I?"

"It's not really the amount of time you spend at it that gets me, Harold. If you spent all that time with one girl it would be different—"

"I know," said Harold. "Then I'd be making love. You can fuck from morning to night and if you're doing it with the same woman it's respectable and its called making love. But if you do it with a different woman every day, it's called fucking and your friends tell you you're obsessed."

"Don't exaggerate, Harold, you don't get laid every day and you know it, certainly not by a different girl every day."

"No, you're right, but I try," said Harold. "I once managed to have a different girl every day for five days. At the end of it I was too exhausted to get obsessed again for a week."

"The trouble is it's destroying your ability to relate," said Spike. "If you'll excuse me for sounding like Nichols and May."

"Nonsense," said Harold. "You can't destroy something you haven't got. My promiscuity is a symptom of my inability to relate. Besides, girls who go down for you the minute you suggest it aren't worth relating to."

"Now, come on, Harold, you can't have it both ways. Why don't you spend some time getting to know a girl who won't go down for you right away, one you like and respect. Who knows, you might fall in love with her, and she with you, and then you could go to bed together and make love and you wouldn't be obsessed anymore."

"I couldn't stand it," said Harold. "I've tried it, and I get too horny."

"Well then, sandwich in your nights of courtship of one particular girl between your nights of promiscuity with a lot of unparticular girls. That way you can have your cake and eat it, too."

"Don't talk dirty," said Harold. "What if I fell in love with her and she doesn't fall in love with me? Think of the agony. Think of the time I would have wasted trying to relate to someone I couldn't fuck when I could have been fucking someone I couldn't relate to."

"Well, let's get to the base of the problem, then, and uproot it."

"Not on your life."

"I'm not talking about your cock, Harold, I'm talking about your boredom. You're bored because you don't like your job, right?"

"I'm tired of being a high-class office boy," said Harold. "It's been going on for a year and a half."

"A lot of guys would envy you, Harold. Stuart Rich has

one of the best reputations in television. Besides, you're much more than an office boy."

"You could give me a title on the door and a Bigelow on the floor, but being assistant to Stuart Rich, famous producer, is essentially being a high-class office boy. The only thing is that you run errands for stars instead of executives."

"But you must be learning a hell of a lot, Harold. I don't see how you could help it. You sit in on the taping of all his shows, don't you?"

"Yes, but I've learned all I can just by watching. I can't learn any more without doing."

"I thought he was going to give you a chance to direct," said Spike, "on that new series next year."

"Oh, he is," said Harold. "Or so he says. But the first episode doesn't go before the cameras for six months, and I'll be assigned one of the very last segments. It'll be nearly a year."

"The trouble with you, Harold, is that you have no patience. You always want to start at the top."

"You're right," said Harold. "It's the bane of my existence, this impatience of mine."

"Well, at least it's a job that feeds your obsession with sex. You meet ten times as many women as I do. That should be some consolation."

"I suppose," said Harold, and sighed. "But I'm tired of secretaries and stewardi and out-of-work actresses. They're all so boring," said Harold. "The secretaries can only talk about their bosses, the stewardi about their schedules and the actresses about their hard luck. I could almost make up the conversation for both of us."

"You're arrogant as hell and inaccurate to boot," said Spike. "What about Laura Bingham? She's no out-of-work actress. She's a big star."

"A theater star, yes. But she's forty-five if she's a day and her thighs are mottled."

"When you first went to bed with her you were boasting about it."

"That's because I was naïve," said Harold. "I mean what would you do if a famous and supposedly beautiful woman asked you to come home with her and screw?"

"I'd pack my basket and go," said Spike.

"Of course," said Harold. "But she's a terrible bitch, and I wasn't really attracted to her, anyway. Most of her beauty comes off with cold cream."

"Then why *did* you go?" asked Spike. "Make up your mind, for Christ's sake."

"Well, in the first place I was flattered, and in the second place I was curious, and in the third place I thought it would be fun to say I'd been in bed with a famous star."

"Those sound like perfectly good reasons to me," said Spike. "A trifle cold-blooded, but then that's show business."

"They were dumb reasons, but just the ones she expects to operate in her favor. Since then I've found out she's been to bed with half the good-looking young men in the city. She never goes to bed with any of them twice, so there's no question of them using her. Instead, she uses them. She makes you feel like a soiled Kleenex when you leave."

"You didn't report that aspect of it the first time I heard the story."

"I was repressing it," said Harold. "Trying to persuade myself that I was glad I'd done it."

"You must have some kind of guilt complex," said Spike, "that keeps you from really enjoying being promiscuous."

"I was afraid you'd arrive at that conclusion," said Harold. "I'd arrived at it myself, but I don't like to have it corroborated by an objective viewer. There are times when I think life is just one big vicious circle."

"You are depressed," said Spike, putting a hand on Harold's shoulder. "You must have had lousy sex last night. Or none at all."

"Oh, it was all right," said Harold. "A stewardess named Jean. There were nine pairs of stockings hanging in the bathroom, but only five of them were hers. The rest belonged to her roommate whose name was Sandra and who was on the Miami-Chicago run for the week. Those stewardi tell you everything. I wish they wouldn't wear so damn much underarm deodorant, though. I swear it turns rancid when they fuck. I don't know whether it's the chemicals in the stuff decomposing, or the fact that it stops up the pores so thoroughly that the sweat turns sour with the effort of getting through the barrier. Anyway, it tastes terrible."

"That's what you get for licking armpits," said Spike.

"What's wrong with licking armpits? Most women have very tasty armpits. It's just stewardi and their bloody deodorants that are a problem. They don't even bother to put the stuff away, it sits there right on the bureau, staring you in the face. New PIT-STOP in the aerosol can, recently endorsed by the wife of some stockcar racer. Jesus."

"Have another drink," said Spike.

"I've already had three."

"Well, maybe you should give up sex for alcohol."

"No," said Harold, "I couldn't do that. I'm a sexoholic as it is. The more I get the more I want."

"Maybe you should abstain for a few days, you might calm down a little."

"No," said Harold. "I'd just jack off instead."

"The trouble with you," said Spike, "is that you have no self-control."

"You're absolutely right," said Harold. "I'm ambitious, impatient and I have no self-control. It makes for a hell of a life."

*   *   *

Harold met Lucy at a party given by one of Stuart Rich's favorite script writers, who lived in a townhouse on West Eleventh Street between Fifth and Sixth Avenues. It was an address that made Harold's ambitions itch, putting him in a surly mood. He prowled the outskirts of the party, from room to room, looking over the women and avoiding the few people he knew. He had developed a shrewd eye for the likeliest bedmates at such gatherings. He could almost always tell, for instance, which women were married: they had a different look about the eyes, a kind of pleasant smugness, very attractive, really, that was different from the kinds of self-assurance projected by unmarried women, no matter how successful they might be. Unmarried women tended to come on harder if they were sure of themselves, or to be even more defensive if they were not. At this party there were quite a lot of married women, and the unmarried women were either artsy types in sandals and flowing hair or elegant types in their thirties and forties who glittered and looked hard. Harold was trying to figure out whether one of the artsy types, who had very blond hair and a protuberant lower lip, was attached to any of the men around her, when a voice spoke beside him.

"She has a very jealous boy friend," said the voice, which was light and musical.

Harold looked around. A girl with short black hair and extraordinarily blue eyes looked back at him coolly. She was very pretty in a pert, hoydenish way.

"Really?" said Harold. "And do you?"

She shook her head and held up a finger in denial. "I wouldn't allow it. I'm a very independent sort."

"My name is Hal," said Harold. "I'm also an independent sort."

"Is Hal short for Harold?"

"That's right."

"I like Hal better," she said. "Sexier."

"I'm glad you think so," said Harold. "We seem to be in perfect harmony right from the start."

"My name is Lucy," said Lucy, with her eyes still on Harold.

"Are you enjoying the party?" he asked.

"No, I'm bored."

"That's good," said Harold. "So am I. Shall we do something about it?"

Lucy smiled. She had very even teeth. "Forward, aren't you? Where do you live?"

"West Seventy-sixth," said Harold and offered his arm.

"Let's go to my place," said Lucy, taking his arm. "It's closer."

Her place was on Charles Street, a floor-through apartment with a separate entrance and a garden. The walls of the large, high-ceilinged living room had been scraped down to the brick, and the room was furnished in modern Scandinavian furniture, all leather and chrome and teak.

"Make us a drink while I put on some music," said Lucy. "Gin and bitters for me."

The bar was almost professionally stocked. There was every variety of liqueur Harold had ever heard of, and at least three different brands of scotch, gin and vodka. "You must be rich as well as beautiful," said Harold.

Lucy looked up from an elaborate console where she was busy adjusting dials. "Rich, no, but I do have independent means to go with my independent ways."

"I call that rich," said Harold, whose mother had just forgotten his birthday. He carried Lucy's drink across to her. "If you're free to do just what you want, I take it you are free to do just what you want?"

"So long as other people don't object," said Lucy, taking the drink with her left hand and groping him expertly with her right.

Harold began to harden at once. The first record fell into place on the turntable. It was, Harold recognized, the "Liebestod." Clearly Lucy was anticipating a (k)night of heroic proportions. In response to this cue, his lance lengthened abruptly.

"I do know how to pick them, don't I?" murmured Lucy.

Harold closed in and placed his mouth on hers. He held his drink behind her back and she held hers behind his. Her mouth was sweet and cool but her tongue assertive. Harold stiffened further, if that was possible, in reciprocal anticipation. He had a theory about women with aggressive tongues. It was a sign that they liked to suck cock. He had not yet had his theory proved wrong.

Lucy suggested that they disrobe. Harold was happy to comply. As soon as he was naked, she went down on him. She had a wonderfully deep and educated throat. He had not measured recently, but at last application of the ruler he had been possessed of seven and one quarter inches at full excitation. Lucy managed to take all of him into her mouth and at the same time extend her tongue far enough to tickle his balls. How she did it Harold could not comprehend, but he found it a thrilling sensation.

"Jesus," said Harold, calling out a name often heard at such moments of extremity even though some earlier and more pagan deity might seem more appropriately addressed.

Harold liked to be blown, but he was not a passive sort, and the ministrations of Lucy's eloquent throat merely increased his desire for the taste of her flesh. He soon raised her to her feet and, beginning with her mouth, began his own slowly descending tongueing of her body. Her armpits, sweet and damp, were happily undeodorized, her nipples, like her nose, had a pert upward tilt, her belly was gently curved, the skin over her hipbones was as smooth as satin but with the warmth of velvet and he laid his cheeks ecstatically against it. The lips of her cunt, veiled by soft curling tendrils of fine black hair, were narrow pink flanges that quivered like some marine creature attached to the floor of the sea.

Harold gourmandized upon her flesh, savoring the subtly shifting textures of her body's surface, the variegated flavors of her body's juices, now sweet, now salt, now faintly bitter, like the taste of cucumber. But she would not let him feast too long without herself partaking of the increasingly generous secretions of his body as it heated to its pleasures. Round and round they went, their tongues each upon the other's body, now gently, now passionately, sometimes with his cock deep within her mouth, sometimes moving slowly against the smooth lubricious gripping of her cunt, round and round on the thick fluffy white rug on the floor of Lucy's high-ceilinged living room, of which Harold's eyes occasionally became aware for brief unreal moments when he lifted them from the more immediate reality of Lucy's body or opened them out of the infinite darkness, round and round, his mind empty of thought, in thrall only to his body's delight, now slow and tender, now fast and throbbing, now thrashing, pumping, panting its way toward some ultimate fusion, or was it fission, racing, every nerve racing together faster and faster toward release.

Harold's balls contracted rapidly, his cock throbbed and leaped, enlarging itself still further, and his sperm spilled out into that night's cunt, which was Lucy's.

Harold lay athwart her, his limbs jumbled, his heart pounding, his cock still hard.

Lucy ran a hand down his back. "You get an A," she whispered. "I don't often give them, but you get one."

"You too," said Harold.

"Yes, I know," said Lucy.

*   *   *

"How many times have you slept with her?" asked Spike.

"Only three times. But for a total of thirteen orgasms."

"That's an unlucky number," Spike suggested.

"Yeah, but fourteen would have been even more unlucky. My cock would have fallen off."

"You must be getting old, Harold. Look, I don't want to be nosy or anything, but while you're on this true confessions bent, can I ask if you're falling for her? Seriously, I mean."

"What would be the point of falling for a nymphomaniac?" Harold asked stoutly.

"Well, it might lead to early impotence, but we don't always have much choice in who we fall for, right? You certainly talk about her enough."

"So? She's fascinating. I mean, how can you avoid talking

about a girl who's fantastic in bed and absolutely crazy out of bed?"

"What do you mean, crazy?" asked Spike.

* * *

One Saturday when Lucy and Harold were shoplifting in Bloomingdale's, a well-dressed young woman careened off a down escalator and clutched Lucy by the arm.

"My God," said Lucy. "Hello, Harriet."

Harold, bemused by the sudden discovery of a silk scarf in his jacket pocket (he had not at first been aware of exactly what Lucy meant by "going shopping"), stood back a short distance. Harriet was quite tall and rather angular. Although the bones of her face were good, in a horsy way, her skin was heavily freckled, leading her to wear too much makeup through which the freckles shone anyway.

"Lucy, how are you, it's been forever, you look wonderful, as trim as ever, how I envy you, I'd heard you were living in Morocco, and somebody, let's see, who was it, Anne Howels, I think, told me you were making a movie," Harriet, breathlessly, said.

"I'm afraid I can't talk about the movie," said Lucy, although Harold was sure she must have started the story herself, at one point or another. So far as he knew, it was a complete fabrication. On the other hand, Harold was learning not to jump to conclusions with Lucy. What appeared true often turned out to be false. And what was originally false had a way of coming true in the end.

"But obviously you're in New York for the moment," said Harriet with a foolish laugh.

"Yes," said Lucy in a voice that sounded suddenly strained. She passed a hand across her eyes, bending a little at the knees simultaneously.

Harriet grabbed her elbow. Harold, dumbfounded, stood and watched. "Is something wrong?" asked Harriet and cast her pale blue eyes, with whites as big as half dollars, at Harold.

Harold stepped closer and put a hand under Lucy's other elbow. It was expected of him, clearly.

"I'm feeling a bit weak, that's all," said Lucy. I've had rather a bad time lately. I have to go everywhere with a bodyguard, it's a terrible bore." She gave Harold a wan smile. "Not that I don't adore you," she said and touched a hand to his shoulder. "If one must have a bodyguard," she said to Harriet, "I can't imagine one nicer than Robin."

Harold, in deference to his new role, straightened his back and tried to look as though he weren't wearing jeans. Who ever heard of a bodyguard who wasn't attired in a dark blue suit with white shirt and striped tie? At least in America.

Harriet's eyes took him in gingerly, as though perhaps his fly was unzipped. "Good Lord," she said. "But what's happened?"

"I was raped by a gang of judo experts," said Lucy, in a low but steady voice.

"Christ," said Harold.

"What?" said Harriet.

"There was this man I met." Lucy lowered her voice still further. You had to strain to hear her. "He was a very rough sort. He wanted me to sleep with him and I wouldn't so he got together a bunch of his friends—they all practice judo, ride motorcycles, wear chains, that sort of thing—and they took turns with me. There wasn't anything I could do." Lucy shrugged, profoundly. "I spent two weeks in the hospital."

"How terrible," said Harriet. But she looked as though she suspected she was being had. Her eyes wavered. She licked her lips. Finally, she appeared to conclude that she didn't have the guts to disbelieve, in case it all turned out to be true. "I'd get out of town, if I were you," she said.

"This is my home," said Lucy with a show of courage. "And Robin will take care of me. Won't you?" she said, looking up at Harold with her eyes full of trust. It was touching, really.

"That's my job," said Harold coolly.

"Well," said Harriet, "do give me a ring some time, when things, uh, settle down. I'm in the book. It was lovely to see you and I, well, I wish you luck, Lucy." Harriet gave Harold a quick smile, using her mouth only, with her eyes averted. She put both hands on one of Lucy's, in a quick patting motion and angled off through the crowd, leading with her elbows, first her left elbow and then her right, fox-trotting toward the exit.

Harold looked at Lucy. She was not even bothering to appear pleased with herself. There was no smile, no hint of self-congratulation. Harold couldn't decide whether once she got into a role she remained stuck there until a new one could be discovered in developing circumstances, or whether this pretense that nothing unusual had occurred was merely another role in itself.

"Who the hell was she?" asked Harold.

"Oh, Harriet," said Lucy, eyeing a counter spread with leather knicknacks. "She was my roommate my second year at Smith." Lucy had remained at Smith only a year and a half, making Harold's three full years at Harvard appear disgracefully long.

"She seemed very glad to see you," said Harold and steered Lucy away from a table invitingly laden with straw belts. He was not in the mood to be arrested, he decided. "At least she did at first."

"Yes," said Lucy, vaguely. "I suppose it's because I used to let her lick my pussy on Thursday nights. It really doesn't pay to do people favors, they always want more."

"Why Thursdays?" asked Harold.

"I had a chemistry lab Thursday afternoons," said Lucy. "It always left me feeling tense."

*   *   *

"I don't think I could fall in love with anyone who wasn't in love with me," said Harold. "I'm not self-destructive enough, in that way at least."

"Perhaps she is falling in love with you," Spike insisted.

"You see her every two or three days and it's been almost two months."

Harold shook his head. "She likes having sex with me," he said. "But she likes having sex with other people in between."

"Then why did she give you a key to her apartment? It doesn't make sense."

"Other people have them," said Harold, making no attempt to explain something he didn't really understand himself but merely accepted.

"Oh, that's great. What if several of you show up at once?"

"I suppose we'll have an orgy," said Harold.

* * *

On her furry white rug, Lucy was rolling around naked with a bouncy-breasted blonde. The strains of César Franck's *Symphonic Variations* filled the air.

"Hello, Hal," said Lucy, raising her head over the belly of the blonde. "This is Mona."

"Hi, Mona," said Harold, unnecessarily loudly.

Mona extended her hand in a universal gesture that seemed entirely out of place. Pocketing his key, Harold managed to saunter across the room and offer his hand in return.

"So you're Hal," said Mona. Her breasts bobbled slightly as she pumped his arm. "I've heard lots about you."

"Really," said Harold. "Like what?" In spite of himself, his voice sounded tense and thin. There were times when he thought he'd never learn to remain absolutely calm in a crisis.

"Well, among other things, Lucy says you've got one of the most beautiful cocks in New York. And she should know."

"I bet you say that about all your boy friends," said Harold to Lucy. It had occurred to him that Mona might be putting him on.

"Are you accusing me of lacking standards, honeybunch?" Lucy's blue eyes flashed at him. Harold fingered the key in his pocket. He had no idea whether Lucy was just teasing or actually annoyed, but he was beginning to think it was a mistake to have exercised his supposed territorial privileges by arriving unannounced.

"Of course not," he said. "I'm very flattered, not to say overwhelmed. It's a big city."

"I thought you were going to say something else there for a moment," giggled Mona. She looked over at Lucy. "Do you suppose I could see it?"

"Why don't you ask Harold? It's his, after all."

"Could I?" Mona floated a ravishing smile in Harold's direction.

"Anything to oblige," said Harold. "Just my cock, or shall I throw in my thighs?"

"Oh, throw it all in," said Mona.

Harold took off his clothes, pitching them over a chair. Having been admired in advance, his member snapped to immediate attention.

Mona let out a small exclamation of pleasure. "Isn't he lovely," she said. "You certainly do know how to pick them, Lucy."

"So I tell myself," Lucy said.

Harold stood around for a while as Mona examined him from a variety of angles.

"Roger should see this," she said, stroking with her plump soft hand.

"Who's Roger?" asked Harold, hoping that whoever he was he didn't have a key.

"My lover," said Mona. "But he's AC-DC. He'd really go for you, I know."

"I'm not much on that scene," said Harold.

"Hal is terribly straight, I'm afraid," said Lucy. "It's his only real drawback. I can't really understand how anybody as good in bed as he is can be uptight about any kind of sex at all, but I guess we live and learn."

Mona got up on her knees and took Harold into her mouth

for a few seconds. She was a bit of a chewer. Releasing him again, she said, "Now what difference would it make if it was Roger's mouth doing that?" she asked, looking up at him winsomely. "I can tell you he's much better at it than me. He says I use my teeth too much."

"I'd still prefer you," said Harold, attempting to divert her with flattery.

"But you're being silly. You wouldn't have to do it to Roger, you know. I mean, I could do it to him. Or Lucy, he likes that better. You might even find you liked doing it yourself if you'd only try. You ought to try everything once, isn't that right, Lucy?"

Lucy nodded. "That's right, love." Her blue eyes rested on Harold's face. Her smile was sardonic.

Harold felt trapped. If there was anything he hated, it was being forced into a choice between doing something he didn't want to do and admitting that he was essentially square.

"Why don't I get to know you better first," he said to Mona. "Maybe we can include Roger another time."

"Oh, wowsy," said Mona.

Harold got down on the rug with the two of them, then.

*　　*　　*

"I hate to admit it," said Harold, "but I don't really like orgies."

"Are you boasting or complaining?" asked Spike.

"People are always asking me that."

"What else do you expect, Harold? Even when you complain about your sex life you manage to give the impression you're getting more than anyone else."

"I can't help it if I have a strong sexual drive," said Harold in a tone of purported objectivity.

"There you go boasting again," said Spike. "I also have a strong sexual drive. I just don't get it out of the garage as often as you do. Anyway, you're a walking contradiction in terms. If you have such a strong sexual drive you ought to like orgies."

"Well, it's strong but it's also fussy," said Harold.

"Strong sexual drives have no right to be fussy," said Spike. "Weak ones can be fussy, it's a good excuse for not going to bed with people and using up your meager reserves."

"Did you teach me to be witty, or did I teach you?" asked Harold.

"Oh, I'm sure it must have been you who taught me," said Spike, with obvious insincerity.

"Anyway," said Harold, "if you could have seen the witch Lucy introduced into the melee on Tuesday, you'd be fussy too."

"What was wrong with her?"

"She was one of those concentration camp types, all chicken bones and no feathers."

"How many of these females are you expected to service, anyway? Or do you have help?"

"That's another problem," said Harold.

"What is?" asked Spike. "That you do have help or that you don't?"

"That I do. If they'd stick to servicing the ladies, I wouldn't mind, but they seem to have this one for all, all for one philosophy."

"That sounds like a good definition of an orgy in the first place," said Spike.

"Exactly," said Harold. "I told you I didn't really like them."

"Why don't you introduce me to the group," Spike suggested. "I promise to keep my hands off you."

"You can take my place if you want," said Harold.

"You going to drop out altogether?"

"I think so," said Harold. "Even when I last saw Lucy alone it ended up leaving me with an unsatisfied feeling."

"I thought she was so good in bed."

"She's fantastic in bed," said Harold. "Or on rug, as the case may be. But that's just the trouble. Her technical facility, shall we say, is so good that I become even more aware of the lack of any kind of emotional equivalent."

"I told you you were falling in love with her."

"No," said Harold. "I'm not. But I have this empty feeling. There are times when I think it would be nice to fall in love with someone or other."

"Harold, my friend," said Spike, "you're a terrible sentimentalist, for a sexoholic."

"I'm not a sentimentalist," said Harold defensively. "But sex by itself isn't enough to make me happy."

"Christ, Harold, you're coming apart at the seams, aren't you? Not even sex with Lucy Supercunt? I know damn well that if you stop seeing her you'll be moaning about how you can't get her out of your head."

"Yes," said Harold and sighed. "I know that, too. That's part of the problem."

*   *   *

The phone rang eleven times before Lucy answered it.

"Hello, Lucy," said Harold.

"Oh. Hello, Harold. You know I hate the phone."

"Yes. I was thinking of dropping by."

"So drop by," said Lucy. "Since when was it necessary to call?"

"I wondered if you were alone," said Harold.

"What difference does it make if I am or not?"

"I would like to see you alone," said Harold. "It's been a couple of weeks since I have."

"Has it?" said Lucy. "I hadn't noticed."

"Would it be possible to see you alone?" Harold persisted.

"I don't run my life that way, Hal," said Lucy. "You know that."

"Yes, I guess I do," said Harold.

"Look, Hal," said Lucy, "why don't we forget this call. A

boy with a cock like yours shouldn't be such a square. You should use it on the world."

"Thanks for the compliment, I'm sure," said Harold.

"Come around when you feel like it."

"All right," said Harold.

"See you, Hal," said Lucy.

"Yes," said Harold.

But he didn't.

6/Renaissance

Harold, who had temporarily run out of comments that might buoy his mother's drifting spirits, noticed the gray-haired lady when she was still some distance away across the Piazza Navona. Twice she circled Bernini's Fountain of the Four Rivers, but her interest did not appear to lie in those huge, airily recumbent representations of the Danube, the Ganges, the Nile and the Plate, nor in their animal cohorts, horse, serpent, lion and crocodile (by intention, it was said, an armadillo), which lurked among the falling waters; instead, her attention seemed to be directed toward the terrace of the Cafe Tre Scalini, where Harold and his mother were sitting.

The lady's surveillance of the café, although obviously intended to be covert, was simply not in the same league, in Harold's estimation, as might be expected of someone more professional, Margaret Rutherford, say, or Dame May Whitty. Along with those two archetypal English sleuths and undercover agents, however, the lady did share a tendency to the haphazard in the shape of her coiffure, which gave the appearance of having been jammed on hurriedly, in the manner of a hat, while going out the door. This particular lady, whom Harold had noticed sidling around the lobby of his hotel the previous afternoon, affected a modified pageboy, of an angular cut that Harold associated with aging lesbian poetesses. It was not a style that went with her small, sharp-featured face at all.

Approaching them at last, the lady ensconced herself at the next table, noisily shifting the metal chairs around. It was eleven in the morning, late for breakfast but early for a drink (although Harold and his mother were having Campari sodas). There were numerous empty tables in both directions; that the lady had chosen to honor Harold and his mother with her proximity was clearly a deliberate act. He was sure she would attempt to engage them in conversation, sooner or later.

Wondering what events, if any, the encounter would initiate, Harold smiled, his eyes sweeping the rich burnt oranges, the flushed pinks, of the buildings lining this most theatrical of piazzas, whose shape exactly echoed the rectangular Roman amphitheater that had once occupied the same grounds, and whose present architecture gave the impression of a series of painted flats that could be whisked into the wings at the conclusion of each day's performance. Perhaps it was the atmosphere of the piazza, perhaps his awareness of having been chosen, for reasons yet unknown, as victim or beneficiary by the gray-haired lady, but Harold had a distinct sense of expectancy.

Here he sat, in a Roman piazza, his own life in flux, one job left behind, with a new professional orientation and, it was to be hoped, a whole new era of his life awaiting his return to New York; while beside him sat his mother, trying (or perhaps not trying—Harold had not really been able to decide) to put her confused life and self back together again, bitter, Harold was sure, about the era she had left behind, wishing it still existed, and fearful, Harold was also certain, that no new era did in fact lie before her, at least not one in which she wished actively to participate.

It didn't bother Harold to be in between things. He

thought, really, that most of one's life was spent in between those moments that really counted, that summed up years of your life or provided a turning point into an entirely different future; and even the significance of those moments sometimes didn't become clear until much later. The trouble was that it was difficult to tell at any given instant whether you were in the trough of the wave, on the way up, at the crest, or on the way down. It was nice, for a while, to be certain that you were in the trough, to relax and enjoy it. He wished his mother could feel the same way. On the other hand, perhaps he was already becoming restless, if he could become so interested in the activities of a furtive old lady, even one with an air of the occult about her.

Harold began to wish, actually, that the gray-haired lady would get on the stick and reveal herself as Madame Sosostris, or whoever she was. Maybe, though, she was wondering if they spoke English, the language in which Harold had heard her order coffee, revealing by her accent that she was American and probably from Boston. English seemed a slightly mundane language for a sibyl to speak, Harold thought; he had been hoping for a Hungarian accent at least.

"It's such a beautiful day," he said to his mother, "I think we should drive out the Via Appia and have lunch in the country. There are several good restaurants out that way."

His mother turned her head toward him, but her eyes slid past his own as she spoke. "Whatever you say, my love."

More than anything else about her, it seemed to Harold, his mother's voice had changed. Its gush and speed were gone, and although both these qualities had often irritated Harold by their presence, their lack was far more disturbing. The mornings were worst. She spoke almost in a whisper, as though unable to shake off whatever nightmares had invaded her sleep. That she had nightmares, he knew. He had arranged, here as in Naples, for adjoining rooms, and he had three times in the past ten days been wakened by the sound of her voice calling out in the small hours, calling somebody's name. Each time she had apparently wakened herself as well, for he had heard her get up and use the bathroom. Harold had kept possession of her sleeping pills, as a rather useless precaution, but she knew that she could ask for one or two if she needed them. She hadn't asked, and Harold suspected that she drank herself to sleep instead—which could easily explain why she was so low in the mornings. Not that she appeared, physically, to be hung over. She was very pale, in spite of the May sun, and there were shadows under her eyes that couldn't really be disguised by makeup. Yet this wanness, this slight look of strain, suited her beauty, setting off her dark hair and large eyes and giving her an odd consumptive radiance. She was looking more and more like Vivien Leigh, Harold thought.

"Excuse me for interrupting," said the gray-haired lady, breaking in at last on renewed silence, "but you sound as though you know Rome awfully well."

Harold's mother was sitting closest to the lady, but until this moment she didn't seem to have taken in her presence. She glanced quickly in her direction, with a startled expression, and then turned back to Harold.

"Fairly well," Harold said. "I was here for a few weeks in 1961, and my mother's visited several times over the years."

"Isn't that nice," said the gray-haired lady, smiling benignly while her sharp little eyes surveyed Harold's mother. "It's wonderful when grown children are willing to travel with their parents, isn't it? So unusual in this independent time of ours. Don't you agree, my dear?"

For a moment, Harold thought his mother was going to ignore the question completely. With her face still to the front, her mouth worked in a kind of wince, as though she had just had an injection. But then she turned toward her questioner and said, "Yes, I do. My son is very much of the times so far as his independence goes, but I've been ill, and he's been very attentive."

"I've been ill myself, so everyone insists, and my daughter thought I should get away. She's really wonderful, a veritable watchdog." The gray-haired lady smiled broadly, revealing that two of her front teeth, at each corner of her mouth, were pointed like fangs. "Of course, they will drag you about dreadfully. I simply refused to go to American Express with her this morning. She didn't want to leave me alone—she's really too devoted—but we absolutely had to get some more money changed. Actually, it's easier for her if I'm not along when she changes money. She lies to me about the exchange rate and pockets the difference. But then, I never was properly generous with her when she was a child, so I suppose I should expect to have her cheat me when I'm an old lady. The young devour their parents, don't they, my dear? Unless, of course, the parents devour them first."

The lady was obviously bats, but she seemed harmless enough. Harold was concerned, though, that her peculiar chatter might upset his mother, who was depressed enough without having to cope with a loony. To his surprise, however, she responded with some spirit.

"I really wouldn't know about that," she said. "There are times when I think I don't understand one thing about human beings." She looked at Harold. "Did I devour you, darling, or are you devouring me?" Her eyes glittered as they hadn't in at least a month. "Oh, dear," she said, fluttering her eyes in almost the old manner, "that does sound rather suggestive, doesn't it?"

"That's all right, my dear," said the gray-haired lady, "we're talking about Freudian questions after all."

"Are we?" said Harold's mother. "How perfectly fascinating."

Harold was astonished. In a few minutes, his mother had passed from introspective gloom to some semblance of her

old self. Yet it was not really her old self, either. The words
were ones he might have expected from her, but she seemed
to be holding herself at a slight ironic distance from them.
Irony had never been one of his mother's strong points, it
had always seemed to go right by her. Or had she merely
been letting it go by, because it suited her purposes?

"My name is Ethel Saunders, by the way," said the gray-
haired lady. "But please call me Poppy, everybody does."

"I'm Caroline Lazer," said Harold's mother, hesitating almost imperceptibly before her married name. "And this is
my son, Harold Hoskins."

"It's a great pleasure to run into you like this," said Poppy
Saunders. "I lost my husband some years ago myself, but
I've never managed to get myself into harness again. Or are
you one of those glamorous divorcées? I keep telling my
daughter she'd make a good divorcée, but she refuses even
to get married."

"Yes, I'm afraid I'm one of those glamorous divorcées,"
said Harold's mother. She gave Harold a slight sidelong
smile, as though to reassure him that she was enjoying herself. Although to anyone who did not know her this smile
would have seemed insignificant, it surprised Harold quite a
lot. It was not the kind of personalized communication Harold was used to receiving from his mother. Perhaps Poppy
Saunders really was a witch.

"I shall have to hold you up to my daughter as an example," said Mrs. Saunders. "If she had some decent alimony,
she wouldn't have to cheat me on the exchange rate, would
she?" Mrs. Saunders glanced across the piazza. "But here she
comes now. Speak of the devil, and all. Don't tell her I know
what she's up to. After all, I'm sure I must be a terrible bore
to her. She deserves a little fun."

Harold looked across the piazza himself. He half-expected
Mrs. Saunders' daughter to be a homely, horn-ribbed type,
perhaps a crypto-lesbian to boot. But there was nothing
homely about the young woman approaching them. Tall,

perhaps five nine, long-legged, slim-waisted and decidedly busty, she was wearing a lemon yellow shirtwaist dress, looking cool and crisp in the gathering heat of the day.

Harold stood up.

"This is my daughter, Marge," said Mrs. Saunders. "And, this is, let me see, oh dear . . ."

"I'm Harold Hoskins," said Harold. "And this is my mother, Caroline Lazer."

"Hello," said Marge, smiling at Harold's mother and then looking back again at Harold himself. Their eyes met, and Harold could have sworn she seemed as pleasantly surprised by him as he was by her.

"Would you like a drink?" asked Harold.

"I'd love one," said Marge. She had a throaty voice with a slight catch to it. "American Express was absolute murder. What's that, Campari soda?"

"That's right," said Harold, pulling out a chair next to him.

"Well, I'd love one of those," said Marge.

*   *   *

On the following day the four of them, at Harold's suggestion, drove to Tivoli and had lunch at a restaurant called the Sirene, which overlooked a waterfall cleaving deep into a green gorge, and where it was possible to choose your own mountain trout live from a swarming tankful. There was another restaurant overlooking the gorge, called the Sibyl, and Harold nearly chose it in secret salute to Poppy, but he had eaten at the Sirene when he visited Tivoli three and a half years before. They had a leisurely meal, concluded by a bottle of asti spumanti. Most of it was consumed by the two older ladies, since both Harold and Marge thought it disgustingly sweet and poured most of the contents of their glasses over the terrace railing into the gorge.

"A libation to the gods," said Harold.

"I hope they don't spit up," said Marge.

After lunch, Harold began driving back out of Tivoli.

"Aren't we going to the Villa d'Este?" Marge asked, rather

sharply. She sat beside Harold in the front seat, her sleek knees showing.

"I thought we'd go to Hadrian's Villa first," said Harold. "Since it takes a good hour and a half to walk around the ruins, out in the sun, I thought it would be pleasanter to cool off in the Villa d'Este gardens afterward. We'll have to retrace our route by a few miles, but we have plenty of time, don't we?"

"You see, Marge," said her mother from the back seat, "you shouldn't be so quick to fault everything. If you behave that way, you'll never catch a man even if you do decide to start working toward some alimony."

"I'll remember that, Poppy," said Marge, casting her eyes to heaven for Harold's benefit.

Harold considered reaching out and clasping one of her knees in a gesture of apparent sympathy, but took out his tactile needs on the stick shift instead.

It was a glorious day. The sky was an absolutely unblemished cerulean blue, and the scattered ruins of Hadrian's vast pleasure palace, rising mysteriously here and there on the green expanses of the plateau, were silent and deserted in the sun.

"Was this where he had his orgies?" asked Poppy, panting a little from climbing over the broken portals of the Maritime Theater. They stood looking at the water lilies floating sedately in the small pool at the theater's center.

"You're thinking of Tiberius," said Marge. "Hadrian was far too refined to take much interest in anything as vulgar as an orgy."

Although Harold tended to agree with Marge's low estimation of orgies, he wondered if her experience was as immediate as his own. He hoped the remark didn't indicate a streak of puritanism. What's more, he doubted its accuracy: Hadrian surely had got up to a little of everything in his time.

Poppy took a strong interest in Marge's comment as well.

"How do you know orgies are vulgar?" she asked her daughter.

"I don't think I'll deign to answer that," said Marge, moving away around the pool. Her cheeks flushed slightly, however, and she avoided Harold's eye.

He went to join his mother, who had wandered over to a cloistered porch that stood remarkably intact among a series of shattered archways. Leaning against a brick column, she gazed back at the pool. "It's lovely here," she said. "So peaceful. It makes me feel very calm. I wonder what it was like when it was first built."

"Full of vicious gossip and vulgar laughter, I imagine, even if not any orgies," Harold said. "Hadrian had an enormous number of hangers-on. Apparently he was taken advantage of very easily after the death of Antinous."

"Who was Antinous?" asked Poppy, loudly, from ten feet away, even though, in her best Rutherford manner, she had given every appearance of not listening at all.

"A Greek boy whom Hadrian fell in love with," said Marge with a staunch expression, as though fully prepared to be challenged again concerning her knowledge of matters sexual.

But for the moment, Poppy seemed more interested in history. "Who killed the poor lad?" she asked, managing to reduce a legend to the status of a boy down the block. For a sibyl, she was grievously uninformed.

"He drowned himself because he didn't feel worthy of the Emperor's love," Marge replied, somewhat oversimplifying the matter in Harold's view.

Poppy contrived a sufficiently oracular tone, at this point, to announce, "Nobody is worth anybody's love."

"I don't agree with you," said Harold's mother, but so softly that she might have been talking to herself. "It's just that we expect too much of people and ask them to be things they aren't."

Harold looked at her. Her eyes were glistening. Only once in his life had Harold seen his mother cry, other than at the theater. That had been on the death of her father. But she did not now release the tears that had seemed to be gathering. "What shall we look at next?" she asked with sudden gaiety, and squeezed Harold's hand.

*   *   *

Half an hour later, after a leisurely ramble through a variety of architectural jumbles, undecipherable pieces of a vast puzzle never to be reassembled, Harold and Marge clambered to the top of the two-story ruins surmounting the far end of the long rectangular pool that was the best preserved and most lovely of the remnants of Hadrian's great palace.

At the other end of the pool, near the statue of Venus that had been the focal point of the surrounding colonnade, Poppy and Harold's mother sat on a stone bench, resting in the shade of an ancient umbrella pine.

"They seem to be enjoying themselves," said Harold.

"I hope so. I really hate to inflict Poppy on anyone, she can be a terrible trial."

"I think it's probably good for Mother," Harold said, not attempting to deny Poppy's peculiarities. "At first I was a bit worried, but it seems to be taking her mind off her own problems."

"I wish Poppy thought she had a problem," said Marge, sitting on a large upended stone. "I had to put her in a nursing home six months ago, after she indulged in a little shopping spree at Lord & Taylor. Just kept going into dressing rooms and exchanging what she was wearing for a new wardrobe, from the skin out. She might have got away with it if she'd been willing to settle for a cloth coat instead of a Persian lamb. But then, Pat Nixon never was one of her idols."

Harold laughed. Marge reminded him of himself at times. "How did Mother latch on to you, anyway?" she asked.

"For once I'm grateful to her. I can tell you, you're way above the usual standard of her pickups."

"Are your compliments always so backhanded?" Harold asked with a smile.

"Often," said Marge. "After all, you were practically the only people sitting there."

"That's true," said Harold. "Though your mother must have spent ten minutes scouting us before she came and sat down. I had a hunch she was going to join the conversation sooner or later." Harold eyed Marge speculatively. "She started off by telling us you were over at American Express changing money and cheating her on the exchange rate."

"Oh, shit," said Marge. "Actually, I wasn't. I thought she might understand Italian money. But I did play a few games with her in Yugoslavia. I didn't think she had any idea what all those dinars were worth. The trouble with Poppy, though, is that she's a lot shrewder than she seems. Crazy, yes, but shrewd. I'd have her committed if I could get away with it. But I'd just end up being cut out of her will and still taking care of her."

"She's probably very grateful to you, in her own way," said Harold, putting one foot up on the stone Marge was sitting on. "Even if she wouldn't admit it."

"Well, much as I hate to admit it, I'm even rather fond of the old bag. In my way."

"I wish I were fonder of Mother," said Harold, lobbing in the general direction of the pool below them a small tile he had picked out of the dirt.

"Aren't you fond of her? You're very nice to her."

"Oh, I suppose," said Harold. "I used to find her almost insufferably flighty and theatrical. On this trip, though, there have been times when she's seemed almost like a real person."

"It's probably just seeing her under different circumstances."

"No, she's changed. About six weeks ago, within a few

days of one another, my father remarried and her husband of the last few years ran off with a Vassar girl. It's practically a comedy, from one point of view, but it didn't strike Mother that way at all. She couldn't stand it all at once and took an overdose of sleeping pills. Fortunately, she changed her mind and called a friend."

"So she asked you to come to Europe with her?"

"No, that was my suggestion. I was about to quit my job and start free-lancing, anyway, and I thought I might as well fit in a vacation while I was at it. Though I would have preferred to pay my own way. Mother insists on taking care of practically everything. It makes me feel like a teen-ager all over again."

"Oh, I'm just overflowing with sympathy," said Marge, sarcastically. "Getting money out of Poppy is like pulling teeth."

Harold couldn't decide whether he was amused or irritated by Marge's rather astringent style. The trouble was that he wanted to sleep with her, and had from the first. There were numerous small indications that she found him attractive, but it was difficult not to take her verbal mocking as a sign of sexual rejection.

"Yes, Poppy made some remark to the effect that she'd never been generous enough with you," Harold said. Thanks to Poppy's chatter he at least had the advantage of knowing a good deal more about Marge than she did about him.

"Did she really?" Marge looked out beyond the pool to where the two women were sitting in the shade. "It's not entirely her fault, of course. Her mother was a real terror, a Victorian harridan par excellence. Poppy never had a chance. She was always a bit loony, as far back as I can remember, and old friends of hers say there was a strange furtive streak to her even as a child. It's only in the last five or six years that things have really got out of hand, though." Marge glanced up at Harold with a rueful smile. "I sometimes wonder how long it will be before I start getting balmy."

"You seem eminently sane to me," said Harold. "If a trifle strong-willed." He met her eyes, and smiled himself.

Marge raised her eyebrows. She looked away and her jaw set into a hard line momentarily. But then it relaxed again, and she merely said, "Well, even if I do go crazy, I will at least avoid passing the affliction on. I have an absolute loathing for children, at any age. A mother myself is one thing I am not going to be."

"Poppy commented on your lack of interest in marriage," Harold said dryly.

"She certainly seems to have covered a tremendous amount of ground."

"Yes, she said she'd often told you what a splendid divorcée you'd make if you ever got married in the first place."

"Oh, God." Marge touched Harold's leg briefly with her hand. "Like her comment in the car. I hope it doesn't upset your mother."

"I think Mother is more amused than anything. Which is a healthy sign. Of course, in another sense, I'm quite sure such comments are made primarily for my benefit." Harold gave Marge a sidelong glance.

"Oh, it's so tiresome," said Marge. "She refuses to understand that if one doesn't want children, and doesn't want or need to depend on a man financially, then one can get a great deal more out of life by remaining unmarried."

"Forever?"

"Probably," said Marge coolly. "But then of course one might always meet some terribly distinguished man with a yacht. One never knows, does one?"

"No," said Harold. "No, *sait-on jamais*."

"I beg your pardon?"

"*Sait-on jamais*? It means 'One never knows.' It's also the title of a film by Roger Vadim. Takes place in Venice. Very romantic and sinister."

"Poppy and I are going to Venice next week," said Marge. "That is to say, day after tomorrow."

"For how long?"

"Only three days. Then back to New York, thank God."

Harold considered. "Mother and I are supposed to go to Venice ourselves, but not until the following week. We could probably change our plans, though."

"Going to follow us about, are you?"

"I don't know," said Harold. "Am I?"

Marge's lips made small puckering motions. "Perhaps," she said. "That might be nice." Suddenly she grabbed his arm. "Oh, God, Poppy's moving around. We'd better get down there."

Harold helped her to her feet and they clambered down the broken stairway into the interior of the ruined building. After the brightness of the day, the cool room at the base of the stairway seemed very dark. Harold took advantage of the dimness to step close to Marge and put an arm around her. She let her weight rest against him, and he kissed her. She responded in a relaxed and exploratory way.

"Shall we have a nightcap together?" he asked. "After the ladies have retired?"

"Yes, I'd like that."

"What time?"

"Oh, Poppy goes to bed fairly early. Say around eleven?"

"Fine. Shall we meet in the bar?"

"No, I hate bars. Would you be scandalized if I suggested coming to your room?"

"Not at all," said Harold, striving to keep any hint of expectation out of his voice.

"Then I'll see you there. Lucky we're in the same hotel, isn't it?"

"It must be fate," said Harold.

"Umm," said Marge, noncommittally, but she took his arm as they picked their way over the rubble on the floor. Emerging into the sunlight again, they scanned the length of the pool. At the opposite end, with her back to them, Poppy suddenly squatted to pee. She was partially hidden from Harold's mother by the statue of Venus, but Harold and Marge had a startlingly clear view of the operation.

Marge covered her eyes in mock despair. Harold could not help but grin.

"You're a big help," said Marge. But then she laughed, quite gaily.

*   *   *

"If you'd met me in New York," said Marge, as Harold removed her bra, "you wouldn't have found me nearly so pliable. At least not so pliable so soon."

"Then I'm glad I met you here," said Harold, weighing her very large breasts in his hands. Some day they would probably sag, being so large, but at present they were simply gorgeous, Harold thought. "What difference is there between New York and Rome?" he asked.

"Europe makes me feel more reckless, somehow. I think less about consequences. In New York, well, you ask yourself, do I really like him enough to have an affair with him, and if the answer to that is uncertain, then you ask yourself if he's really sexy enough to be worth going to bed with just once and feeling distressed about it afterward." Marge moved her shoulders around, pushing her breasts against his hands. She smiled into his eyes. "Besides," she said, "I was horny."

"Is that so," said Harold. "Funny, so am I."

Harold was entranced with Marge's body. Her shoulder and hip bones had a good peasant bulk to them, but her arms and legs were long and slender with surprisingly fine wrist and ankle bones.

"You have beautiful hands," said Harold.

"Is that all?" said Marge.

"Far from it," said Harold. "But I thought I'd begin with the details and work up to the whole."

"Start with the whole," said Marge. "You can fill in the details later."

"Well, if you insist," said Harold. "I think you're gorgeous all over."

"That's more like it," said Marge. "You're quite a hunk yourself."

Unfortunately, however, the bed creaked. In fact, it made an unholy racket. "Christ," said Marge. "It sounds like a garbage collection at dawn."

Harold, reluctantly, slowed his rhythm. "Pretend we're in the country and it's a farmer sawing wood on the other side of the hill."

"Your mother's right in the next room, isn't she?"

"Mother knows the facts of life. Besides, she's probably drunk herself to sleep by now."

"All right," said Marge. "The hell with it. In America I'd be embarrassed. In Rome, who cares? I'll try to moan loud enough to cover that awful scraping sound. It gets on my nerves."

Harold grinned. "Are you noisy? Good. So am I."

The Roman night during the next half hour was increasingly rent by the sounds of metal squeaking against metal and of wood protesting against weight and movement, as well as by the moans of Marge and the groans of Harold, both of whom, in tribute to Roman beds and European romance, abandoned themselves thoroughly to their cause, to the point where the incredible noise they were making became an integral part of the whole experience, exciting in itself and an additional goad to pleasure. Their intensity increased, they relished each other and ravished the quiet, the noise grew greater, they writhed and pounded, and just at the moment of most intense feeling, as their senses crested, the springs dropped three inches within the bedframe.

If anyone had put it to him in the form of a question, Harold would have said that it was impossible to laugh and come at the same time, but the moment the bed dropped, although his balls were still contracting and the sperm still shooting out of him, Harold, together with Marge, dissolved simultaneously into helpless idiot laughter.

*   *   *

"Good morning, darling."

Harold's mother was sitting by the window, painting her nails a bright coral shade. Depressed though she might be, she had not in any way neglected her appearance over the past several weeks. Her nails, her hair, her makeup were as carefully tended as ever, and her choice of clothes as fastidious. It did seem to Harold that she sought out mirrors less than she once had, approached them with a more practical and less rapt expression, but that he could not take as anything other than a change for the better, a sign that she was adjusting to the facts of age. Not that he really felt she should be too distressed about it, for even in her mid-fifties she was a very beautiful woman.

"How are you today, Mother? Did you sleep all right?" Harold had asked this automatically, and immediately regretted it. In view of the uproar he and Marge had created in the still of the night, it seemed an injudicious inquiry.

His mother glanced at him briefly, and then looked back at her nails. There was a half smile on her lips. "As well as ever," she said. "I hope you'll forgive me, my love, if I say I'm glad you and Marge are getting on so well. I was afraid the trip was proving a bit of a bore for you."

Harold could not help grinning. "Thank you, Mother. I was having a very pleasant time, in fact, but I will admit that it is now even more pleasant, if a bit noisy."

His mother did not look up. "I did hear you laughing, I must admit," she said with consummate tact, holding one hand at arm's length to examine her nails. "It's odd, you know, but Poppy and I were discussing you two out at Hadrian's Villa yesterday, while you were up on that parapet for so long."

"And what did you conclude?" asked Harold, genuinely interested to know.

"Well, to begin with, Poppy wondered if you and Marge might get together. We agreed that you would make a most handsome couple, and then Poppy asked me if you were good in bed."

A few months ago, Harold was sure, his mother would have let this remark fall without emphasis, giving no indication of being aware that it was unusual. But now she glanced up at him once more and smiled mischievously.

Harold laughed. "Good God. What did you say to that?"

"Well, I assured her that I lacked personal experience in the matter, but as that had always been one of your father's most considerable, if rather unexpected, virtues, I wouldn't be at all surprised if you'd inherited it. Poppy seemed to find that an adequate answer."

"She's a mad lady, isn't she?"

"Yes, but she's rather happy in her madness. And she's good for me right now. I find her amusing and at the same time I'm able to pity her. It makes me feel a good deal better."

Harold was silent for a moment, and then said, "Perhaps you wouldn't mind, then, if we changed our schedule and joined them in Venice for a few days. They'll only be there a short while before going back to New York."

"Whatever you like, love. It really doesn't make too much difference to me, you know, at the moment."

Harold did not know quite what to reply, but his mother set the bottle of nail polish aside and looked up at him. "I'm sorry, darling. You're being very good to me, and I don't want you to think I'm unappreciative. It's just that I'm not really very good at living on hope, or looking toward indefinite futures. I'm afraid I'm very selfish and self-indulgent, but I need satisfaction at each moment. Tomorrow has never been a word I've cherished."

It was sad, Harold thought, that he liked his mother so

much better, felt a genuine fondness for her even, when she was unhappy. He took the few steps to her side and leaned over to kiss her cheek.

"I can't embrace you, darling," she said. "My nails."

* * *

Dear Spike,

Venice is just as I expected it to be, and, in spite of the fact that it's a different season of the year, just as it appears in Sait-On Jamais. *The reason that film is so much better than anything else of Vadim's is obviously the city itself. I almost feel as though I've been here before and fully expect to see Robert Hossien around every corner. I would be more carefully on the lookout for Françoise Arnoul, or her equivalent, but I've got my hands full on that score as it is. In fact, Mother and I came here a week early in order to continue in the company of a crazy (literally) old lady and her exceedingly nubile daughter, whose name is Marge. Marge you will be meeting before long, back in New York, where she lives when she isn't hauling her mother around on a short leash. Oddly enough, it was the mother, a lady with a definite aura of the occult, who brought us together. Marge, aside from being a gorgeous creature, is a very independent one, almost as splendidly cynical as you or me, totally uninterested in marriage (no, she's not putting it on, her mother is after her about it a good deal of the time), and generally down on sloppy emotional involvements. In other words, just the girl for me in my present state of mind (long may it persist). Her only drawback (thus far revealed) is that she's so determinedly anti-romantic as to find Venice merely campy, a sort of old-world version of Disneyland. I cannot agree, and must say that I have yet to discover a more satisfactory background noise for making love (screwing, excuse me, the atmosphere is getting to me, you can see) than the lapping of an occasional boat along the canal outside your window at three in the morning.*

Even Mother appears to be finding romance in Venice. She's met a Greek ship owner, replete with yacht, upon which she may even sail off into the Adriatic sunset if she doesn't play it too coy. The gentleman is not in the Onassis class, of course (for which let us be thankful, my mother and Miss Callas would not hit it off, I'm sure), but nevertheless owns some fifteen ships. At a million bucks a boat, that should keep him in ouzo. What's more, he's charming, so charming that I checked up on him a bit, all Mother needed at this point was to be taken in by some Mediterranean gigolo out for the American dollar. He appears to be entirely on the level, however, and is fast rescuing Mother from her glooms. Just when I was getting to like her some, too. But that's another story, one that can keep until I get home. It has a heavy moral about asking people to be things they're not, which, would you believe it, is a quote from Mother herself. She had a fit of self-knowledge in Hadrian's Villa, astonishing me a good deal and perhaps herself even more.

Anyway, I'm looking forward to returning to NYC, and getting my ass in the free-lance sling. Marge will be back there before this letter reaches you and if Mother's Greek comes through with an invitation for her to go cruising on his yacht, as seems likely, I may skip back a week early, with only a stopover in Paris for nostalgia's sake.

So I'll see you in ten days perhaps, two weeks at most. The moral of this letter is: never be rude to spooky old ladies, they may have daughters named Marge. Which is spooky in itself, I could say some things about my growing belief in the sanctions of fate, but maybe it's just the effect of being in a city with streets of water. It would be difficult not to believe in fate here, Marge notwithstanding.

As ever,
Harold

7 / Mortality

O<small>N</small> the second Tuesday in March of 1966, Harold, who was depressed enough as it was, went to an expensive Italian restaurant in mid-town Manhattan and had ground glass for lunch. It came in a bowl of *pasta e fagioli* soup—as a kind of garnish, perhaps. As he bit down on a mouthful of the soft, succulent beans, the tender pasta, Harold's teeth crunched against something that was hard and rough-edged but which he could feel breaking into smaller pieces as his teeth came together. A small pebble of some sort, he surmised: Harold had begun to do a good deal of cooking himself, of a fairly elaborate sort, and he knew the problems that dried beans could present in the way of gravel.

His expertise, however, proved inaccurate—which seemed to be happening to him more often these days. Managing with considerable grace to spit out the offending particles into his spoon, he was stunned to discover that he had been chewing on a piece of glass; indeed, he had plainly bit it in two.

"There's glass in my soup," he said in bemusement.

His guest at lunch, Mrs. Charlotte Green, looked up from her antipasto in alarm. "Glass?" she said.

"Yes. Look." Harold held out his spoon. There among the

half-chewed beans lay two unmistakable pieces of glass, each about a quarter of an inch in length, approximately the size of the little green and black tranquilizers nestling in the antique silver pill box in Harold's breast pocket. Two unmistakable pieces of glass. They appeared to be rough all around, as though they might have come from the shattered stem of a wine glass. A perfectly feasible explanation, Harold thought, but however satisfying to the intellect, not really very good for the nerves.

Charlotte Green had paused with her fork in mid-air, precariously balancing a chunk of tuna fish. "Did you swallow any?"

Harold's stomach questioned itself uneasily.

"I don't think so," he said.

"You should eat some bread, I think," Charlotte suggested as she guided her fork the rest of the way to her mouth.

"Yes, I suppose I should," said Harold. He reached out and tore off a piece of crusty Italian bread from the half loaf in the bread basket. Biting off a hunk, he began to chew, and was appalled to find himself grinding more glass against his right wisdom teeth. Then Harold did an exceptionally stupid thing, by his own judgment. Instead of rinsing his mouth with water and spitting out the entire mess, ground glass and all, into his soup bowl, he merely pushed an additional lump of bread between his teeth, chewed and gulped it down.

"Now I have swallowed some," he said.

"Oh, dear," said Charlotte. "I do hope you're going to complain."

"Waiter," called Harold. The waiter was passing quite near, but in the manner of his profession was staring straight ahead, his hairy ears tucked in against themselves, well insulated against anything less than a shout—a shout which most customers could be expected to withhold for fear of attracting the censorious attention of the diners at the next table, and the next. He would come only when convinced that he had demonstrated his complete equality with any and all capitalist pigs and fellow democrats. From his days as a bar boy, Harold well understood the mentality.

Depressed though he was, Harold was not to be cowed by such tactics, and shouted. As if on cue, the participants at the three nearest tables craned and stared.

The waiter swiveled, smiling. Smiling? Harold, taken aback, neglected to press his advantage and said in a much more subdued voice, "There seems to be some glass in my soup."

"Glass?" The waiter's voice could not have achieved a tone of more total disbelief.

Harold retrieved the two shiny pieces of evidence from his bread and butter plate, where he had deposited them. He displayed them in the palm of his hand.

Like a nervous fence, the waiter appraised them. Then he smiled again, but only with his teeth. He held out his hand, glancing around toward the front of the restaurant. "If you please, sir."

Harold dropped the two bits of glass into the waiter's extended palm. The love line was short and crooked but the life line was long. The waiter's fat fingers closed over the evidence, and he turned away.

"I should have kept a piece," Harold muttered.

"Exhibit A," said Charlotte Green.

But the waiter proceeded directly to the maître d', who looked sharply around toward Harold's table. Harold raised an eyebrow. The maître d' hurried across the room. He was short, but handsome, in a flashy middle-aged way. "Where did you find this?" he asked in an unnaturally floured voice.

"In my soup," said Harold succinctly.

The maître d' stammered slightly. "Really? I can't understand it."

"I didn't bring it with me," said Harold, striving for hauteur but achieving only sarcasm.

The maître d' had swarthy skin, well tanned from an apparently recent winter vacation. Harold hadn't had a vacation since he turned freelance. He didn't even own a sunlamp, which was the more likely explanation of that dark, healthy glow. At any rate, he was pleased to see the maître d' flush an even darker color. "No, no, of course not, I, well, it just isn't the kind of thing that happens here, you understand."

"It looks like a broken wine glass to me," said Charlotte in her most gravelly voice. "Perhaps you have a Russian in your kitchen. I'd check on it, if I were you."

The maître d' gave a strangulated giggle. "Yes, quite, I, sir, I hope there was no damage?"

"I think I swallowed some of it," said Harold.

The maître d' looked terribly distressed. His Adam's apple worked. "You did?"

"Yes, I'm quite sure I did." Harold was quite proud of the calm with which he spoke. He even felt quite calm. Tranquilizers were wonderful things, really. He had already miscalculated, however. The maître d' seemed to be taking this exceptional calm as a sign that Harold, all forgiveness, was letting him (to say nothing of the restaurant) off the hook. "Well, I hope there are no further consequences, sir," he said, beginning to sidestep. "Let me know if there are any, uh, medical problems."

"I certainly will," said Harold with dignity.

"Well, then, very good, sir. I'm terribly sorry about this." And he wheeled away, knocking against a table (empty, unfortunately) in his haste, and racing toward the kitchen. Harold didn't think he had ever seen a maître d' move so fast.

"Did you really swallow some?" asked Charlotte Green.

"A bit," said Harold, bravely.

"Well, I shouldn't worry. The human body is a remarkable thing."

"I hope so," said Harold.

"Just keep yourself filled up. It will pass right through."

"I hope so," said Harold.

"I thought you were extremely calm about it. Most men would have been yelling their heads off."

"That was cowardice, not calm," said Harold. "I should have yelled and screamed and threatened suit."

"I'm glad you didn't. Hysterical men are so tiresome." Charlotte Green speared her remaining anchovy and popped it in her mouth.

Harold ate another piece of bread. "They might at least have offered me a free drink," he said. "Am I just getting crotchety as I approach thirty, or is the world a worse place than it was ten years ago?"

"Probably a little of both," said Charlotte, and patted his arm.

It was ironic, really, Harold thought. There you were, making a nice gentlemanly gesture, taking a production assistant to lunch because she'd been a big help to you. Not a young, sexy blond thing, either, with whom you could play kneesies, but dear old Charlotte Green, a widow in her fifties, a pleasant gray-haired lady with a mind like a UNIVAC; one of those indispensable women who knew more about certain practical aspects of the business than the men who earned five times as much for bossing her around, himself included. Dear old Charlotte Green. Harold had just finished directing a driver training film commissioned by the U.S. Post Office. A brilliant artistic success, of course, with a jump cut from a pothole to a broken axle that would take Pauline Kael's breath away. Charlotte Green, however, had helped make things bearable. So he had taken the nice old bag to lunch. And what did he get for it but a plateful of glass.

"Oh, come now, Harold, don't exaggerate," said Ron Bigelow, who had been the producer of the Post Office epic.

Harold had an after lunch conference with him to talk about their next project, for a California gas company.

"It only takes a very little bit to seem like a plateful, when it's glass," Harold insisted.

"Listen, Harold," said Ron, tilting back in his fancy aluminum and leather desk chair, a Christmas present from his rich wife, "the human body is a pretty remarkable thing."

Why don't I have a rich wife, Harold thought. Of course he did have a rich mistress, now that Poppy had been successfully incarcerated. But would Marge give him an aluminum and leather desk chair? Not bloody likely.

"Stop brooding," said Ron.

"I'm not brooding," said Harold. "I wasn't even thinking about ground glass. Maybe I should have my stomach pumped out," he added.

"Oh, for Christ's sake."

"Actually," said Harold, "I think I'd rather die than have my stomach pumped out."

"Stop worrying about it, Harold. What's a little ground glass? My sister's kids have swallowed pounds of it."

"They have?"

"Sure."

"And nothing happened?"

"Of course not."

"None of them had his appendix out?"

"Yeah, two of them, I guess."

"Probably caused by the glass," said Harold, who wasn't much interested in living long enough to film a fleet of gas trucks anyway. "They say grape seeds can cause appendicitis, so surely ground glass would be even more efficacious."

"Harold."

"Yes."

"Do you even have an appendix?"

"It was taken out when I was thirteen," said Harold, and sighed. "Sometimes they grow back, I'm told."

"Let's get some work done, shall we, Harold?" Ron Bigelow tilted and swiveled impressively in his expensive chair. Harold got up and went to the door.

"Where are you going, Harold?"

"I'll be back in a minute. I need another tranquilizer," said Harold.

*　　*　　*

At the local liquor store that evening the clerk extended his sympathies and recommended taking a laxative. The glass would just slide right out, he maintained. He smiled as he asked Harold to hand over the tax on his bottle of scotch. Harold invariably put down merely the advertised price of the bottle, in exact change, as though the tax simply didn't exist. It was a kind of standing joke between himself and the liquor dealer. Harold liked having a friendly relationship with the neighborhood storekeepers; it make him feel as though he weren't living in New York, although he couldn't have said where else he would have liked to live if given a choice.

Harold looked forward to gathering in the sympathy of the drugstore clerk as well, but when he got there he found that the man behind the counter was someone he'd never seen before. It seemed a bad omen to Harold. And, in fact, the clerk looked aghast when Harold related his saga. He wrapped up the package without looking at what he was doing, his eyes fixed on Harold as though on a ghost. He didn't say anything, really, but his eyes brimmed with horror. Not a born pharmacist, Harold could tell.

"Harold, I don't care," said Marge, her voice sounding very thin and far away.

"The man at the drugstore looked at me as though he knew the posse was waiting for me at the end of the street."

"Harold, I have the flu," said Marge. "Asian flu, maybe even Siamese. I told you not to call. I feel horrible and I need all my sympathy for myself. I'll phone you at the end of the week."

"I may not be alive at the end of the week," said Harold.

"I'll send a dozen daisies," said Marge, and hung up.

Sometimes Marge made Harold tired. He supposed that he loved her, but they never said such things to each other. Harold occasionally wished that they did, or could, wished for a woman he could openly, sloppily love, and who would shamelessly cherish him back. Short of that, he'd settle for Marge and a script that called for actors instead of gas trucks as its principal characters. Clearly, life was defeating him.

On the Sixth Hour News, there was a report on the latest advances in artificial kidneys. So what if Harold didn't have an appendix? He still had two kidneys, a bladder and a urinary tract. The glass could lodge anywhere, causing who knew what varieties of pain and infection, necessitating operations, convalescence . . .

Harold decided to get a grip on himself. Hypochondria had been rising in him lately like the Ganges during the monsoon. He poured himself another scotch and managed to become sufficiently exercised about the latest reports on the war in Vietnam so that he practically forgot about what he himself was busy digesting, or trying to digest, in the way of foreign matter. For dinner he ate both halves of an avocado, a small steak, creamed onions and what must have been almost a pound of mashed potatoes. Marge would be asking him where his washboard went and stop comparing his abdomen to Paul Newman's, if he didn't watch himself. That was another sign of age. He was becoming vain. It pleased him to have his abdomen held up to Paul Newman's by way of comparison, even if Marge was only half-serious. Sometimes he pretended she was Joanne Woodward, but he didn't tell her about it. He could just see Marge as Orson Welles' daughter in *The Long Hot Summer*, standing there saying she was no little rabbit.

After dinner, Harold went to a W. C. Fields revival and forgot all about his insides. Harold enjoyed W. C. Fields immensely. He even felt that they had something in common, though he couldn't have said exactly what aside from a general aptitude for cynicism. But, somewhere within Harold's thin soul, he was sure there was a fat man with a bulbous nose clamoring to get out. Harold laughed a great deal and nearly lost his scarf. A middle-aged lady from the same row caught up with him in the lobby and gave it back to him. For a second he thought it was Poppy, escaped and at large in New York. "Thank you," said Harold. "Just like my son," said the lady. "He got married, though." Harold grinned uneasily and exited into the winds of March.

It was on the subway going home that he began to think about ground glass again. Curious, Harold observed to himself, how the subways stimulated the anxiety syndrome. Or not so curious, rather. Harold recalled the rubber-wheeled cars on some lines of the Paris subway, that moved through the tunnels with only a pleasant whoosh to record their passage. If only all his days might pass in a pleasant whoosh. He should have checked his horoscope for the day, before venturing to reward Charlotte Green for her existence; perhaps it would have warned him off. Harold did not take his horoscope very seriously, but every now and then it did come up with a prediction of startling accuracy, the perfect camp guide to the intelligent failure's lack of success in love and art.

The subway screeched and jerked to a stop at Harold's station. He retrieved himself from the all too willing lap of the young man next to him and ascended out of the caverns into the cold. As soon as he got home, he looked up his horoscope, capitulating to superstition.

"Tuesday, March 14: Difficult. You may feel entirely too expansive and can easily bite off more than you can chew. Your judgment may be faulty, and you should avoid unusual expenses. Work may be delayed through health problems or the affairs of older people."

"God," said Harold, aloud, and quickly checked for Wednesday the 15th:

"Good. Daily affairs and routine matters will probably run easily, without opposition. Correspondence can be handled with imagination. Friends will be less contrary than of late. It is a somewhat dull day but one that is free from pressure."

That was reassuring, at least. Free from pressure and no mention of health problems. But, Christ, if he'd read his horoscope for today, he would never have scheduled that luncheon. On the other hand, how was anyone to guess that biting off more than one could chew referred to pieces of glass. Thousands of people, even hundreds of thousands, perhaps, must possess the same paperback horoscope of the year. And whoever had concocted it, he (or she, more likely) surely hadn't considered ground glass as being one of the things one could bite off too much of.

All the same, Harold felt with a neurotic twinge, it was disturbing. A good horoscope for tomorrow meant nothing. The internal ravages effected by today's lunch might not make themselves known for weeks, months even.

Harold groaned and went to the kitchen to make himself a nightcap. He would have to remember to say no more about it to Marge. Let her bring the subject up (if she should so deign) and then pass it off as nothing at all. Once she had recovered from her oriental sniffles she'd be unmerciful about such hysteria on his part. It was ridiculous, anyway. The glass would simply slide right out. Nevertheless, Harold reminded himself to take a dose of the laxative he'd bought, before going to bed.

*　　*　　*

Half an hour later he pulled back the covers, feeling pleasantly tired and sleepy. Harold had become something of an insomniac lately, even sometimes when he spent the night with Marge, and memories of ground glass between the teeth were not, he suspected, any guarantee of a restful night. But as soon as he had stretched out in bed, sprawled on his stomach, he decided that, ground glass or no, he would have few problems this night. He drifted slowly, deliciously downward, slowly deliciously downward—

Ground glass.

The thought flew upward, like an escaping air bubble.

Ground glass.

Harold wriggled his head deeper into his pillow, as though to block his ears.

Ground glass.

Harold resisted. Harold thought about Marge. Harold thought about Marge's marvelous breasts. But that was no good, that was just another way not to get to sleep, when she was absent from his side. Harold knew from experience.

Harold turned onto his left side.

Ground glass.

Harold began to take a series of deep breaths, emptying his mind. You are very sleepy, he said to himself. You are very tired. You haven't a thought in your head. You are very sleepy and you haven't a thought in your head.

Ground glass.

Harold recalled that in some concentration camps the Nazis (or was it the Japanese?) used to feed the prisoners only once a day to insure that their stomachs would be empty, and then filled their evening mush with finely powdered glass. The glass was too fine to be filtered out of their systems, and it passed through their intestines into the rest of their bodies, into the bloodstream, destroying them slowly, torturously from the inside; and not knowing why they were in pain, why they were dying, they went on eating their evening mush, their powdered glass.

Harold had read about it. It came back to him now.

Ground glass.

How fine was the glass that Harold had swallowed? After

all, he'd ground it between his teeth (Harold's jaw worked in reflex, and he felt a cringe run through himself), had ground it finer; he himself had ground it down. Why hadn't he spit it out, the whole mess into his soup bowl? His parents may have failed to provide him with any larger scaffolding against which to frame his life, but they sure as hell had taught him manners. Better to die like a gentleman than live like a boor.

Ground glass.

Harold resisted. He called upon logic. You would have to feed someone an awful lot of ground glass before it could really do much damage. Besides, if he was to go by the Nazis, it was important for the stomach to be empty. Harold's stomach certainly wasn't empty. He'd even finished his lunch—a large portion of *saltimbocca alla romana*. And there were all those potatoes he'd consumed at dinner. Creamed onions. A whole avocado.

Ground glass.

Harold sat up in bed, furious with himself. This was absurd. He got out of bed and went to the kitchen, scuffing along in his broken-backed slippers, which he kept only in order to annoy Marge. Some day maybe she'd break down and buy him a pair herself, with a few dollars of Poppy's money.

Harold heated some milk in a saucepan, watching it bubble and steam at the edges. Harold poured it out into a mug, added a huge shot of scotch, and sprinkled the whole thing with nutmeg.

Ground glass.

He couldn't take another tranquilizer, he'd exceeded his self-imposed daily limit as it was. And he didn't have any sleeping pills. He couldn't take barbiturates, they left him feeling muddleheaded for half the next day; and the over-the-counter brands never worked. Harold swallowed his hot milk. Barbarous thing to do to scotch, really. Not that it tasted bad. Harold rather liked it, in fact. Marge was the one who thought it was barbarous. She was probably right. Marge was usually right. Unsympathetic bitch.

Harold padded back down the hall to his bedroom. He told himself he should sue. Why had he been so calm, letting the restaurant off the hook that way? Charlotte Green would testify. Fifty thousand dollars for mental anguish. I can't sleep, judge, I keep wondering when one of those little pieces of glass is going to lodge some place, work its way through into a vital organ, obstruct my urinary tract, eat a hole in my liver, cause a cancerous growth. Harold could feel the unnatural cells forming around the sharp little particle, malignant and spreading. Dead at thirty from ground-glass cancer.

God damn it, he would sue. Just to cover himself. Why not? Who could say when or how one of those nasty little bits of shattered wine glass would make itself known in sudden excruciating pain. Couldn't even see it with X rays. They'd have to cut him open and feel around. Knives, blood, pain, daisies from Marge.

Harold slumped on the edge of his bed.

Clearly, the pressures of modern living were getting to him. "Stop it, Harold, just forget it," he said aloud. Wiggle your toes, feel them relax, feel the scotch warming you, feel the muscles relax. Feel yourself calming down, Harold, feel yourself getting sleepy.

It was cold sitting on the edge of the bed. Harold didn't feel himself relaxing, not very much. Harold got under the covers and thought about Marge. Harold hadn't slept with Marge in four days. Harold jacked off. It was the only way.

Harold's body relaxed. Harold felt his body relaxing. His legs tingled as the tension drained away. Harold turned on his side again, curled in upon himself. Harold let his mind float away.

Ground glass.

Harold let his mind float away. The night was dark, the sea lapped the rocks, he sat on a high parapet and the water

broke below, there was a moon, the earth looked flat, the
water glimmered, the sky was a bowl over the flat water.
The night grew darker. The sea lapped more quietly at the
rocks below him. The rocks below him.

And then, abruptly, brutally, like falling onto those rocks
below, Harold was wide awake.

Harold was terrified.

There was no one thought in his mind, no one particular-
ized thought. Just an apprehension of terror, absolute terror.

Ground glass.

It was as though he were imploding upon himself, becoming smaller and smaller, gathering into himself with greater
and greater force until, he knew, there would be only one
infinitesimal dot of pure terror that must then explode outward again into—nothing.

Harold had not known before.

Ground glass.

Oh, everyone knew. Of course. With their minds, everyone knew. But Harold, who had known with his mind, had
not known like this before. Really known, with all of his
being, with the whole of his thin soul. Never truly compre-
hended that it would, must, happen some day, and that he
was not prepared to face it.

Harold heaved himself up in his bed, sitting very still in
the enclosing blackness. Gradually his eyes adjusted to the
dark and his ears opened themselves to the sound of the
midnight city.

Harold sat breathing in the dark.

8/Peace

HAROLD, who had been trailing his hand idly across Marge's body with a calm, almost abstract stroke, suddenly began to feel horny again. It wasn't unusual for Harold and Marge to make love more than once in the course of an evening, but, on this occasion, as his cock rose along Marge's thigh, she sat up abruptly and stretched out her hand for her cigarettes. Harold's cock could, of course, manage to make itself hard long after he had reached the point of satiation by any other yardstick, and the mere fact of erection was not to be taken, necessarily, as an indication of immediate, panting desire. Still, Marge had reached for her cigarettes just a moment or two before the action would have constituted an outright rebuff, and Harold was hard put to hide his annoyance.

Marge lit her cigarette and took a deep drag on it. "Are you still going to that march tomorrow?" She looked down at Harold through a haze of smoke, speaking without any particular emphasis. This was old ground.

"Why?" asked Harold, sighing. "Are you going to come with me after all?"

"Of course not. I wouldn't waste my time."

"You're just lazy," said Harold, and was unable to resist running his hand along the inside of her thigh.

"Go to hell," said Marge.

Harold withdrew his hand. "You brought it up again, love. I don't care whether you go or not. I just wish you didn't care that I was going."

"I don't," said Marge, scattering ashes along his forearm.

"Then you must want to make damn sure I understand how much of a fool you think I am. For a girl who's always going on about everyone being allowed to do his own thing, you're awfully quick with the scorn."

"I'm just registering my opinion," said Marge. "It's not as though I were stopping you from doing anything."

"Of course not. Like the Momma who can't stand her daughter's fiancé and says, 'Go ahead and ruin your life, I'm not going to interfere.'"

"I thought you were just going to a peace rally, Harold. I didn't know you were getting married."

"God forbid. I have enough trouble with a mistress, or whatever you are." As Harold was well aware, mistress was a word Marge found galling in the extreme.

"Oh, I don't know, Harold," she said, with the bile rising in her voice. "Now that you're getting so successful in television, maybe all you need to complete the picture is some adoring little simpleton of a wife whose existence revolves completely around you."

"I find it hard to imagine what that would be like—being adored by a woman," said Harold. "Perhaps that's because I have so little experience of it."

"So sorry to disappoint," said Marge with pride. "But I'm sure there are lots of sweet young things out there who'd be happy to have you make up all the rules. Poor deluded creatures."

"Why don't you start a movement?" Harold suggested derisively.

"It's already under way, darling," said Marge, and blew smoke in his face.

Harold lay down on his back and shut his eyes. It was

only recently that this kind of debate had penetrated into the bedroom. Marge had never been willing to let any statement she disagreed with go unchallenged, but in their first year or so together such exchanges had usually been good-natured. The undertone of irritation had developed so gradually that they didn't even notice—and then one day it took over completely, becoming the dominant note. It was no longer possible, when they disagreed, to dissolve their differences in laughter. Harold blamed himself in part; he had become so frustrated directing endless industrials that he'd let that frustration color the rest of his life. Now, even though things were finally going well for him professionally, it seemed to be too late to recapture the insouciance that had once existed between Marge and himself. They had both allowed their self-esteem to become involved, and acrimony over the dinner table had become a habit. It wasn't that they argued constantly; there were many things they agreed about, and sometimes an entire evening would pass in peace. Harold couldn't have stood constant bickering, yet now that they were turning recrimination into a bedroom sport, he looked with foreboding along the worsening way to that end.

"I'm tired," Harold said, with his eyes still closed. "Let's forget this idiotic conversation and go to sleep."

"You can go to sleep. I'm going to read for a while."

Harold sat up in exasperation. "You know I can't go to sleep while you're reading. If you want me to go home, for Christ's sake, say so."

"I don't want you to go home, Harold. But I'm not sleepy. I want to read. And I'm not going to lie awake for an hour in the dark while you snore away in preparation for some ridiculous peace march." She picked up Susan Sontag's *Death Kit* off the bedside table and brandished it about.

Harold shook his head and gave a short laugh. "You know I don't snore," he said. He reached out and patted Marge's knee. "I'd better go home."

"If you prefer."

"Jesus God," said Harold loudly.

Marge sighed. "Sorry," she said, laying the book in her lap. She took a deep breath. "I guess I'm being difficult."

Harold clasped and unclasped his hand on her leg. "We don't seem to be doing very well these days, do we?"

"I guess not." Marge would not look at him, however.

"Sometimes," Harold suggested gingerly, "I think we're too much alike."

"Maybe. Or too different. And I'm not trying to contradict you, either. It's possible to be too alike and too different at the same time."

"I suppose it is." Harold kissed Marge on the forehead. "I'll call you," he said, getting up out of her bed. "In a couple of days."

"Yes. All right."

Marge watched him for a moment as he began to dress, and then her eyes dropped back to the book in her lap. She began to thumb through it, looking for her place.

*   *   *

The previous fall, Harold had been to another peace rally, where he had been informed by one impassioned speaker that his presence put him, along with the rest of the crowd, in the vanguard of history. Actually, he felt more like a camp follower. Marge's scorn had led him, as too frequently happened, into a more ardent espousal of the faith than he really felt. Not that Marge's contempt for the peace movement indicated any hawkishness about the war: in spite of a few personal qualities of the big-beaked variety, Marge would certainly have flocked with the doves in the great aviary of life. She was simply contemptuous of politics in general. For the past two and a half years she had been celebrating Lyndon Johnson's ultimate adoption of the Goldwater policies of escalation with a litany of I-told-you-so's. Marge was unconvinced that it was possible to control the direction of governments even by voting; a few thousand demonstrators, it seemed to her, could hardly pack any more wallop than two fleas on an elephant.

Harold didn't really have a much higher opinion of politicians or of the democratic process than Marge did. Nevertheless, some corner of him continued to indulge itself in the romantic notion that it was possible to change the world and improve upon the past, to believe that since some men were indubitably wiser and stronger than others, the ordinary citizen had a duty to encourage the actions of the wise and the strong, over those of the foolish and the weak. But his basic skepticism always reasserted itself in time to rescue him from any such extreme as ringing doorbells for candidates or selling buttons on street corners in the name of peace. Participation in a mass demonstration was about as far as Harold was willing to go in expressing his moral superiority.

Looking around him at the crowd gathering at the intersection of Fifth Avenue and Ninety-fifth Street, Harold decided that a majority of the participants were, like himself, sunshine moralists. The late spring day, balmy and beautiful, had brought out large numbers of young women pushing baby carriages. Their presence, Harold had no doubt, was as much due to the weather as to any passion for peace. Their dedication to the sun was of course much more valuable, in a public relations sense, than even the most fervent moral commitment of the several hundred young people in beards and beads. Young mothers, like senior citizens in cardigans with leather patches at the elbows, looked good on television.

A goodly contingent of baby carriages also had the effect of reducing the number of obscenities shouted from the sidelines by that brave sort of American male who had spent the best years of his life in exotic foreign lands, killing people and screwing the local prostitutes (always in ample supply in countries receiving American assistance in the running of their internal affairs, Harold had noticed). Since these stalwart ex-soldiers on the other side of the police lines owed the best fucks of their lives to the American war machine, Harold could certainly understand that they would support LBJ's adventures in Vietnam, if only out of a spirit of sentimental reminiscence. Nevertheless, they had been known to reminisce rather violently, at the expense of other peace marchers, and Harold determined to keep close to the baby carriages for the greater safety of his skin.

"Would you be interested in a McCarthy button, sir?" asked a voice at his elbow.

The inquiry was made in the politest of voices, but Harold could have done without the "sir." Hell, he wouldn't be thirty for six months yet, and he doubted that even then his youth would vanish overnight. Harold sometimes thought that most of these kids in their late teens and early twenties would lose their sense of identity completely if you took the generation gap away from them.

"I'm afraid I'm not a fan of the Senator's," said Harold.

The young man's mouth had a petulant cast. He was the kind of kid who, in Harold's college generation, would have had to draw on all his reserves of courage to try out for the yearbook staff, yet here he was telling America at large where its moral responsibilities lay.

"I suppose that means you're for Bobby Kennedy." The young man's voice took on a surly edge.

"Well, let's just put it this way," said Harold, "I'll take ruthless over phony any day."

"What's that supposed to mean?" The young man was definitely getting angry.

"Just an intuition," said Harold. "And don't hit me, it would be bad for the Senator's image."

"Oh, go to hell," said the young man, and stalked away.

A few paces to one side a girl wearing a Kennedy button on her bright blue blouse smiled at Harold. He smiled back and shrugged. "I guess that kind of exchange is one reason why the peace movement isn't taken more seriously," he said.

The girl nodded. "I'm afraid so. But still I think your intuition about Mr. McCarthy is exactly right."

"Phony?"

"Definitely," said the girl with a grin.

She was quite slight, although clearly not flat-chested. Her light brown hair was worn long, but held back by a ribbon in an almost schoolgirlish way, and there was something trusting in her long narrow face, some quality of innocence that made her seem very young.

"How old are you?" asked Harold, suddenly curious.

"I'm twenty-eight," she said, blushing.

"Not that I have any right to ask," Harold added apologetically.

"That's all right. I'm not ashamed of my age—yet."

"Well, I'll be thirty this fall, just to give you a fair information exchange. And equally unashamed. Or so I tell myself."

Their conversation was interrupted by the march organizers exhorting the crowd to form ranks, to follow the instructions of the parade marshals, and at all costs not to get involved in violent incidents. Lyndon Johnson, it was suggested, should be allowed to maintain the patent on credibility gaps.

Harold was glad to have some company and fell into step alongside the girl in the blue blouse. He'd never really expected to persuade Marge to come along, but he'd originally thought that both Spike and his latest girl, Barbara, would march with him. But then Spike had asked Barbara to marry him, so they'd ended up traveling to Baltimore for the weekend to visit her parents. In fact, if Marge hadn't been so caustic about it all, he probably wouldn't have bothered to come by himself. He hoped he could insinuate himself into range of television camera; with any luck Marge might see him on the Sixth Hour News, marching happily along beside his pretty companion. On the other hand, maybe that wasn't such a good idea—Marge would just say she knew there must be some reason besides a love of peace to inspire his attendance. With Marge, you really couldn't win.

* * *

"Peace now," the crowd chanted as it marched down Fifth Avenue. "Peace now." The sky was a clean washed blue, and the new leaves on the trees along the Avenue stirred in the spring breeze. Harold felt his earlier pessimistic mood lift as he walked briskly along. "Peace now," he chanted, and had a sense of being one with the many who strode before him and followed after in the long column. He raised his voice, chanting louder. "Peace now."

But already a new cry was going up, cutting sharply through the buoyant air. "Hey, hey, LBJ, how many men did you kill today?"

Harold did not join in this new and strident cry. In fact, only about a third of the marchers did take it up. Harold was walking only a short distance behind a large group of "Mothers for Peace," three out of four of whom pushed their carriages before them like identification badges. As the "Hey, hey, LBJ" slogan was taken up, they lapsed briefly into silence, and then went back to a chant of "Peace now." Only two mothers took up the separate and more militant cry, and one of those fell quiet again almost immediately. The other was marching only a short distance in front of Harold and diagonally across from him, so that he was able to see her quite clearly. She had a rapt, beatific expression on her face, like a statue of St. Theresa being ravished by the Holy Spirit. She was not, obviously, wearing a bra under the button-down men's shirt that was tucked into her denim wrap-around skirt. Oblivious to the curiosity (as well as some overt hostility) she was arousing in the women around her, she swung rythmically down the street, chanting her rude question to the President in a loud flat voice.

Harold, turning slightly, inclined his head in unspoken comment to the girl-woman wearing the Kennedy button, who was walking just to his right.

"If I were Lyndon Johnson," she said, "that phrase would just make me more determined than ever to prove I was right."

"I'm sure that's exactly what it does do," Harold agreed. "Moral outrage can be pretty obtuse."

"Yes," said the girl, and sighed. "Sometimes I feel as though I'm trapped between a bunch of right-wing yahoos on one side and a bunch of left-wing ones on the other. But then that makes it sound as though I'm equipped with better judgment than anyone else, which really can't be true."

"Oh, I don't know why not," said Harold, smiling. "I've been convinced for years that I'm more sensible than practically anybody. That's not to say that I'm terribly sensible, it's just that standards are awfully low."

The sound of a new rallying cry arose behind them. "Ho, Ho, Ho, Ho Chi Minh, You Win, You Win, You Win." Along the right-hand curb, outside the main body of marchers, a guerrilla force of hippies in headbands and yards of beads double-timed its way toward the head of the parade. The leader carried a Vietcong flag, held belligerently aloft. "Ho, Ho, Ho Ho Chi Minh," cried his followers as they advanced past the more docile majority of marchers. A parade marshal was keeping pace with them, futilely trying to persuade the flag-carrying leader to lower his flag and fall back into line.

Harold and the girl with the Kennedy button had both turned their heads to watch the advance of these insurgents; now, just as the flag carrier began to move past them, he was attacked from the right-hand curb by a group of young toughs who suddenly vaulted the police lines. The toughs tore into the flag carrier and three of his followers with such force that they were knocked sprawling into the main body of the marchers, creating a violent chain reaction. The girl with the Kennedy button was marching directly to Harold's right, quite close to the outer edge of the column. Knocked off her own feet, she caromed into Harold with an impact that threw him to the ground. As he fell, he tried to catch himself, but all he managed to do was scrape his left arm from the elbow to the wrist.

The girl landed on top of him, momentarily knocking the breath out of him. Other marchers gathered around them as they lay on the pavement. Somebody helped the girl to her feet, but she immediately knelt down beside him again. "Are you all right? I'm so sorry." She looked close to tears.

Harold, who still couldn't speak, waved his hand in a gesture indicating it was all right. He swallowed, trying to draw air back into his lungs. "I'm okay," he wheezed, sounding anything but. "Breath knocked out."

He sat up gingerly, and the girl and a couple of other marchers helped him stand.

"Oh, you're bleeding," said the girl.

Harold looked down at his arm. It was beginning to sting. He had had his shirtsleeves rolled up to just above the elbow, and a good deal of skin had been removed from his arm. It was dripping blood very theatrically, although none of the cuts seemed to be too deep.

The parade, which had come to a halt behind them while the police broke up the fight and hauled off the participants, now began to move forward again around the small disaster area where Harold was standing in the middle of the street. His arm suddenly began to hurt like hell.

"Maybe we should get over to the side," suggested the girl.

"Yes," said a worried-looking young man with a marshal's armband. "We ought to get you some first aid."

"I'll be all right," said Harold, with a show of bravery. "Though I think maybe I'll call it quits on agitating for peace, at least for today."

"Look," said the girl with the Kennedy button. "You really should do something about that arm. I live only about five blocks from here. Won't you let me clean it up for you? I'm accident-prone, so I have a full medicine cabinet."

Harold looked at her, and then glanced around at the street sign. They were standing at the corner of Eighty-fourth Street. The fastest way to get home to his apartment would be to cut across the park. "Well," he said, "that's very nice of you, but don't you want to keep on with the march?"

She made a face. "No thanks," she said. "Sometimes I wonder if it's all worth saving anyway."

"The country, the world or the human race?"

"The whole miserable race," said the girl. She gave a sudden laugh, her eyes lighting up mischievously. "My name, by the way, is Hope. Hope Richardson."

"Mine is Harold," said Harold. "Although I really like to be called Hal."

"Hal what?"

"Oh, sorry. Harold Hoskins."

"Hello Hal," said Hope.

*   *   *

Harold winced as Hope washed his arm. Not that she wasn't doing a good job; her fingers were very deft and as gentle as could be expected considering the amount of dirt that had to be scrubbed out of his stripped flesh.

"Are you by any chance a nurse?" asked Harold, even though he was quite sure she was not. The glimpse he had got of her apartment, before being hustled into the bathroom for first aid, indicated a more intellectual profession. One entire wall was taken up by books, floor to ceiling, and the remaining walls were covered with what appeared to be old-master prints and drawings.

"No," she said. "But thank you for the compliment. Actually, my father's a doctor."

"You've clearly inherited his skills."

"Only a very small amount. He's a brain suregon."

Harold glanced down at Hope's hands. They were narrow and graceful, with long, tapering fingers.

"All right, now, this is going to sting a little," she said, taking up a bottle of disinfectant.

Sting it did. "Ouch," said Harold, manfully.

"Be over in a minute. I'm only going to put Band-Aids on the parts that are still bleeding. The rest of it will heal more quickly if it's open to the air."

"Whatever you say. I certainly wouldn't have done such a good job."

Hope smiled at him. "Well, it's the least I can do, after knocking you flat."

"It was hardly your fault," said Harold.

"You know, it's ridiculous to think I went out there today to cheer myself up, persuade myself that it was possible to help change things."

"One of these days the whole system is going to collapse," said Harold, with a vision of doom reinforced by his own pain. "To have a democracy you have to give your citizens reasons to trust the government and put faith in the law. I think a great many people are becoming less and less sure they can bring themselves to do either one of those things and more."

"I'm afraid you're right," said Hope, relinquishing his arm after a final inspection. "I think that'll be all right now. How about a drink to repair our good spirits?"

"Well," said Harold, hesitating. "Maybe I should be going along. I don't want to impose."

"You're not imposing. I need a drink, after that experience, and I'd rather have it with company."

"Okay," said Harold. "Then I'd be delighted."

Hope replaced the Band-Aid box in her neat-looking medicine cabinet. "I'll leave you to wash up. What would you like to drink?"

"I'm not fussy. A beer, gin and tonic, scotch—whatever's available."

"How about a vodka and tonic?"

"Better still."

"Lime?"

"Lots of lime," said Harold.

Hope smiled at him and left the bathroom, closing the door behind her.

Harold peed, thinking how delighted Marge would be to see his wounds. He'd have to play up his rescue by Hope. "A Florence Nightingale of decided charm," he whispered as he shook himself off.

When he came out of the bathroom, his drink was waiting for him. A half lime floated in it, making it look doubly cool and refreshing.

"Thank you," said Harold, as Hope handed him the cold glass. "To being rescued by fair maidens."

For the second time that afternoon, Harold saw Hope blush. She seemed to blush surprisingly easily for such a calm, efficient young woman.

"To peace marchers," she replied. "Or some of them, anyway."

"I like your apartment," Harold said, looking toward the large windows at the far end of the room. "You get a good north light, don't you?"

"Yes. I'm not usually here in the summer, so it's more important to have good light in winter."

"Are you an artist?" asked Harold, looking around at the walls. "Or just a collector?"

"Oh, I dabble a bit. But I'm mostly a collector. I have professional excuses, though. I'm supposed to be an art historian."

"How impressive."

Hope made a face. "It may sound that way, but believe me, I'm not a very impressive member of the profession. I enjoy the research, just for itself, and it does get me to Europe every summer. But I loathe having to write it all up."

Harold was charmed by Hope. He felt immediately at home with her. It would be nice, he thought, to have a female friend. Marge was something between a friend and a wife, without really being either. Most of the other women he knew fell into one of three categories: women with whom he worked but did not see socially; the wives of friends, none of whom had tried to make him a confidant, perhaps because they knew of Marge's existence; and girls he was interested in for their bodies alone, of which there had been a greater number lately than any time since he'd met Marge. A woman who was a friend would make a nice change.

"Is your arm bothering you?" asked Hope.

"No, it feels much better. I'm sorry, I was thinking about some work," Harold lied.

"What do you do?"

"Well," said Harold, "I guess you'd say I was a film director. But only for television, so far."

"Now, that really is impressive," said Hope.

Harold felt a warm glow, which he did his best to ignore.

"Would I have seen anything you've done?"

"Possibly. I did a couple of experimental plays for NET last year. And one of them, believe it or not, led to doing an episode of "Run for Your Life.""

"Oh, I believe it," said Hope. She gave a small laugh. "Or shouldn't I?"

"Well, it was kind of a freak chance," said Harold. "One of the NET plays was about a child prodigy who's kidnapped, and the same kid who played the part was hired for "Run for Your Life," to play a child prodigy who runs away when the pressures get too much for him. Anyway, the scheduled director got badly cracked up in an accident just before they were to begin shooting, and the producer had to get someone else fast. He called a couple of old reliables, who were busy, and then decided to give me a chance since I'd worked with the kid before. He had a first-rate cameraman, and it was primarily an acting show instead of an action one—that particular episode, I mean—so he figured he could take a chance on my lack of experience. Since then I've been pretty steadily employed. Next season I'm supposed to do a CBS

Playhouse, if the idiot writer ever finishes revising the script and CBS doesn't junk the whole project."

"It would terrify me to be part of a profession that depended that much on luck," said Hope.

"Sometimes," Harold admitted, "it terrifies me, too, but I think some luck comes everybody's way. You just have to be looking for it and be ready to take advantage of it."

It occurred to Harold that he wouldn't have said or believed that a year or so earlier. And he wouldn't have believed it in spite of the fact that he'd already had one lucky break in his professional life, when that hotel had exploded in front of his eyes on the rue Dauphine. That had been almost seven years ago now, which seemed incredible. Two real breaks in seven years. But at least he was now in a position to make his own luck, by sheer hard work, if not by sheerest native brilliance.

He tilted his glass, which was almost empty.

"Would you like another drink?" asked Hope. Her own glass, however, was still half full.

"No, thank you," said Harold. "I should really be on my way. But speaking of luck, may I take advantage of this afternoon's by suggesting supper and a film some time soon?"

"Oh." Hope looked startled.

"I don't mean to intrude on your life. I mean, if you'd rather not, I'd understand perfectly."

Hope blushed. "No, no. It's not that at all. Yes, I'd like to go to a film."

"Would next Thursday be all right?"

"Yes, that would be fine."

Harold knew that Marge already had an engagement for that evening, which would prevent any complications from arising. For some reason, he didn't think he would tell Marge about his Florence Nightingale after all. Not just yet, anyway.

"You've been wonderful," he said to Hope. "If it weren't

for you I'd probably still be dripping blood through the streets of Manhattan."

"You should change the dressing tomorrow," said Hope.

Harold stood up. His arm gave a twinge as he put pressure on it. "I'll see you Thursday, then. Will six thirty be all right?"

"That's fine," said Hope, smiling at him. "I'll look forward to it."

"So will I," said Harold.

And they shook hands at the door.

9 / Corruption

O^N their first evening together, Harold and Hope went to see *Elvira Madigan*, which they agreed was pretty to look at but rather puerile. Young girls were weeping all around them, however, and it made them feel old. Hope wore a green dress and insisted upon paying her own way. The green of her dress, a subtle dusty color like the undersides of leaves turning in the wind, changed the color of her eyes. Harold had remembered them as blue, but they were on this occasion a definite green. It kept one's interest up, Harold thought.

On their second evening together, they went to see *Rosencrantz and Guildenstern Are Dead*, which they both enjoyed immensely, in spite of the fact that sitting behind them were two ladies from the Bronx who insisted upon discussing the varying attributes of different makes of television sets throughout the first act. Hope's eyes had gone back to blue, complementing her silk dress of that color.

On their third evening together, Harold discovered that Hope's eyes not only changed color according to what she wore, but that they had a circular speckling of gold toward the inner rim of the iris. Harold surmised that this ring of barely visible brilliance surrounding the dark pupil might have something to do with the look of perpetual surprise that gave Hope's eyes their particular charm—aside, of course, from their changes in color. Harold noticed the gold specks only because he was seated next to her on a banquette during dinner, and was looking at her from a new oblique angle in just the right light.

"It's the same angle from which you can most easily tell if someone's wearing contact lenses," said Harold. "I know. I had to abandon a shot on 'Run for Your Life' because the angle revealed that the leading lady guest star was wearing them. It took all the glamour out of her French accent."

"Tell me," said Hope, "who gets to sleep with leading lady guest stars? The leading man or the director?"

"Usually neither," said Harold, somewhat taken aback. "At least not when her husband's along—or her lover, as was the case with the lady with the French accent."

"And if she's on the loose?" Hope persisted, smiling.

"That depends on the woman. The beautiful but empty-headed ones tend to fall for equally empty-headed actors. The insecure ones are drawn to directors, who love to play Svengali anyway. If an actress has intellectual pretensions, and looks down on Hollywood, she's likely to fall for a writer. Then, of course, there are the clever little gold diggers, who go after producers because they have the most money. The smartest ones of all marry oil millionaires or foreign princes and quit the business altogether."

Hope seemed very amused by this catechism. She was a very rapt listener, a quality that Harold liked in women. He found that it made him feel that much more witty, and thus perhaps caused him to be that much more witty.

"Do you have all that written down some place or did you just make it up?" asked Hope.

"Oh, it just came rolling off the tongue," said Harold. "That's not to say that any of it's true, of course."

Hope laughed. "I see. And when an actor or producer or director goes about seducing an actress, does he know enough to choose the right type? Or haven't they all thought it out as carefully as you have?"

Harold wondered what conclusions about him Hope was drawing from all this. He was quite sure that some were being drawn. "Most of them probably haven't thought about it at all," he said. "They just go after what seems available. But I think instinct is pretty good about such things, most of the time. Don't you?"

Hope gave an enigmatic little twist to her head, and looked down at her drink. "I suppose," she said. "I'm rather surprised any of them get married at all," she added, looking up at him again.

"Well, there's still a good deal of public pressure to get married. That's changing, but not as fast as you might think. Besides, I think most of them get married in perfectly good faith, believing it's forever. Which may be silly of them, and naïve, but they're not so different from other people, really. If you gave John Doe the opportunities for infidelity that are open to most show business people, you wouldn't find him hesitating for long. And of course he's able to afford a divorce instead of just doubling his intake of rye."

Hope was looking at him with great attention, her lips slightly pursed. Harold wasn't used to such scrutiny. Marge never tried to understand what made him tick; she simply wasn't interested. There were things she liked about him and things she disliked, but she didn't care to pursue the matter further.

"You're a funny combination of things, aren't you?" Hope said.

"Am I?" asked Harold. "Do I want to be?"

"Well, you're very cynical but you're not hard. That's unusual, I think."

"I don't think I like the sound of it," Harold said with a smile. "Cynical but soft. Sort of like marzipan, sugary but bitter. Harold, with heart of marzipan."

Hope laughed. "You make it sound awful. Actually I meant it as a compliment."

"Oh," said Harold. "Let's see then. Like a coconut, perhaps. Break me open with a hammer and you'll find me running with the milk of human kindness."

"No, that's not it, either," said Hope. "It's not as though one thing was inside the other. They're sort of woven together. That's what's different. I mean, there are probably a lot of people who are nasty on the outside and sentimental deep down inside some place. But that's not you at all."

"Well, that's a relief at least," said Harold with terrific seriousness.

"You're teasing me," said Hope.

"Yes, but actually I think you're very perceptive. I just don't like to be found out."

It was true, Harold thought, that she was perceptive. But it seemed to him more than casual perception, the kind of insight that indicated more than usual interest and more than usual thought. It was possible that he was merely being vain, which would hardly be a new thing, but he suspected that her curiosity about the sex life of the stars was connected with an unspoken (perhaps even an unrecognized) curiosity about his own sex life.

Sex was not something they had even really discussed. In keeping with his desire to form a friendship with a woman, he had avoided thinking of Hope in terms of sex. It wasn't that he found her unattractive; on the contrary, he thought she was very lovely. He simply wasn't very curious about what she was like in bed. Or at least he hadn't been curious. The more he thought about the fact that he wasn't curious, though, the more he decided that he was probably beginning to be. Or was that just because he'd decided that she was curious about him?

Harold was confused. "What would you like to see this evening?" he asked, getting back to particulars.

"I don't know, have you seen *The Fox*?"

"Yes, but I'd like to see it again."

"Don't be silly. There are lots of things around."

"No, I'd seriously like to see it again. It isn't great, or anything, but it does have some really wonderful moments. Besides, I have this thing about Anne Heywood."

"It sounds as though I'd better be sure to like it, too."

"No," said Harold. "If I insisted on my friends liking the same movies I do, I'd have to give them up altogether."

"Which?" asked Hope. "Friends or movies?"

"I don't know," said Harold. "That's exactly the decision I wouldn't want to have to make. So I try to be tolerant instead."

In fact, Harold was very curious to hear Hope's reaction to the film, and he knew perfectly well it would affect his opinion of her. Marge had hated it, guided by the outrage of Pauline Kael. (Miss Kael was so convinced that good movies could not be made from good literature, however, that she hadn't even managed to report accurately what had happened on the screen in front of her, as Harold had pointed out to Marge with considerable satisfaction.)

"A complete distortion of Lawrence," Marge had hissed.

Harold had never come across any two people, let alone critics, who could manage to find the same meanings in any of D. H. Lawrence's hazily evocative works, and he didn't really understand how you could distort something that had no defined shape to begin with. Marge, however, had apparently discerned a very definite shape in Lawrence's novella, and was furious not to find it intact on the screen. Harold had countered with his own firm belief that books and movies shouldn't even try to achieve the same things, in spite of the fact that they might be working with the same characters, plot structures and themes. But Marge was not interested in abstract debate. She adored Lawrence, and felt he had been defiled.

Harold sighed, perusing the list of appetizers balefully; only two of them were going for less than $1.50.

"I think I'll have the vichyssoise," said Hope.

Harold smiled at her. Not only was that one of the two items under $1.50, but it had been commended in a review in the *Times* that Hope had mentioned reading. She was still insisting on paying her own way to the movies, but had given in on the question of the dinner check. It impressed Harold that her general common sense should carry over even into the ordering of meals she wasn't going to be paying for. He'd taken out too many young women who, misunderstanding the attributes of class, immediately zeroed in on the most expensive dishes on the menu and then only picked at them because they were too rich and too fattening. On one notable occasion, a creature of particular physical but few other charms had even added insult to robbery by announcing that she'd always hated chicken livers and nobody was going to put anything over on her by calling them *foie gras truffe de Strasbourg* (which she managed to mispronounce in its entirety, including the "de") and charging a lot of money for them. Harold had offered to trade her his avocado, but she didn't like avocados either, they were too slimy. Harold hadn't even been angry: it was just what he deserved, he told himself, for organizing his evening (stretching on into life) around unmitigated lust.

"What are you thinking about?" asked Hope.

"How much I enjoy having dinner with you," said Harold.

"Really? I was wondering if you were bored, you looked so far away."

So Harold told her about the chicken livers, and didn't even try to disguise his reasons for taking that particular young lady out to dinner in the first place.

*   *   *

Although he wasn't sure whether he was being turned on by the presence of Hope sitting beside him in the dark or by the voice, eyes and sensual self-awareness of Anne Heywood up on the screen, by the time Sandy Dennis had been felled by her tree and Keir Dullea had packed Anne Heywood off to the joys of the straight life, Harold was feeling pleasantly horny. It was the first time he had felt horny while with Hope, and he thought that he liked the feeling.

Hope took his arm as they emerged onto Fifty-seventh Street and, informing him that she loved the movie, especially Anne Heywood's confrontation with the fox itself in the frozen snowy woods, she dragged him a few doors toward Sixth Avenue to peer at the expensive toys for grown-ups that glittered in the windows of Henri Bendel.

"Henri Bendel," said Harold, "is the kind of store that makes me understand the appeal of Communism. Anyone who would shell out $24.95 for a desk calendar has got to be living off other people's sweat."

Hope looked amused. "I'm sorry you feel that way," she said. "I was going to ask you back for a drink. But perhaps I'd better not, my bottle opener cost me $6.95 at Bendel's."

"There's a world of difference between a calendar and a bottle opener," Harold quickly allowed. "A calendar just reminds you that there are three hundred and sixty-five days of problems in the course of a year, whereas a bottle opener helps to assuage the pain of that awareness."

"Besides," he said, wielding the item in question on a bottle of soda a few minutes later, "I think your bottle opener is exceptionally handsome. Well worth the price."

Hope, who had her head in the refrigerator looking for cheese, withdrew long enough to smile at him. There was something about Hope's face that caused her smile to transform it to an unusual degree, from vulnerability to mischievousness. Harold paused for a moment with the bottle of soda in his hand, continuing to look at Hope after she had stuck her head back in the refrigerator.

Harold poured the soda. "Shall I take the drinks out to the living room?" he asked.

"Yes, do," said Hope, closing the refrigerator door with her elbow, her hands full of cheeses wrapped in foil.

Harold took the glasses out to the living room, but after he had set them down on the coffee table, he turned around and went back into the kitchen. Hope was arranging the cheeses on a plate with some crackers. Going up behind her, Harold put a hand on each of her shoulders. "That looks good," he said.

"Umm, I think so, too."

Harold, with a sudden impulse, turned her around and kissed her.

Harold considered himself, in a slightly self-mocking way, a connoisseur of kissing. He had never known two women who kissed alike, and there were times when he wondered if the ways in which women kissed were not as distinctive as their fingerprints—a concept he thought could do a lot for police morale. Yet he had to admit, reluctantly, that you couldn't tell by the way a woman kissed what she would be like in bed. Some women who kissed wonderfully turned out to be curiously inhibited in bed; they seemed to be concentrating on their kissing in order to forget what was happening to the rest of their bodies. There were others who kissed horribly, like rodents, constricting their mouths and pushing their tongues at you as though trying to drink out of a thimble. But sometimes they turned out to be stupendous lays.

Hope kissed marvelously, her mouth at once relaxed and responsive. Harold hoped that she would be one of the special kind of women whose kisses did reveal the quality of her love-making—because he was suddenly aware of her in a new sense, and wanted her, wanted her surprisingly much.

But he did not want to hurry things, and after a few moments he let her go. There was a slight smile on her lips, but her eyes were serious. She held his gaze briefly, reading his expression just as he was reading hers, and then she turned and picked up the plate of cheese and crackers.

They moved out into the living room, neither of them

speaking, and they sat down on the sofa, half-turned toward one another. They picked up their drinks.

Harold raised his glass slightly. "To lucky meetings," he said, as lightly as he could.

Hope raised her own glass and repeated his words, but in a softer, more tentative voice.

Harold felt distinctly odd, curiously self-conscious. He felt as though he were on a swiftly rising emotional escalator, yet he couldn't have said at just what point its ascent had begun. Harold wasn't really used to mixing sex and emotion, not even with Marge. It was one of the reasons, he thought, why he was so good at getting women into bed: he was able, quite coolly, to weigh the situation and to seize, quite consciously rather than intuitively, the proper instant for taking the initiative. Now he felt unsure, unsteady, off-balance. He was afraid to push too far too fast. The situation was controlling him rather than the other way around.

Before he should become paralyzed by self-awareness, Harold set his glass down on the marble-topped table and reached out to take Hope's glass from her. Her face was serious without being grave, feminine without being meek, and open without being overtly seductive.

Harold had once taken a glass from a girl in this way and dropped it, spilling its contents, which had unhappily consisted of a Bloody Mary, all over the girl and her couch. The memory of that incident suddenly assaulted him, but he managed even so to convey Hope's drink safely aside.

He leaned forward and began to kiss her once more. Gingerly, he moved his hands, softly exploring. Hope's own hands touched him, moving along the outsides of his thighs, then her arms went around him and he could feel the deft strength of her fingers against his back.

Harold began to fumble with the buttons on Hope's blouse. He had got four of them undone when she stopped him.

"I'd hate for you to think I was forward," she said, "but

this sofa reminds me of the back seat of a Nash Rambler. I suggest we shift locations."

Harold sat back, laughing, relief and excitement surging simultaneously.

Hope continued for a moment to recline where she was, smiling at him and yet scrutinizing him too, once again. Then she got up, quickly and gracefully, and held out her hand to him.

Harold got up and went with her into the small but cheerful bedroom. The walls were yellow and there were dark green drapes at the windows. The room had a warm, intimate feeling to it. He had not been in it before.

Until this evening, Harold had not kissed Hope on the lips, and now she was walking naked into his arms. Perhaps it was the way she did that, walked naked into his arms; perhaps it was the particular feel of her skin against his or the mingled sweet and musky smell of her warm flesh; perhaps he had been in love with her for weeks, only now to be surprised by the joy of it—but whatever it was, whatever mingling of instinct and longing that caused his heart to jump, his skin to tingle and his cock to leap, whatever it was that caused the tenderness and the lust in him merge into a single feeling stronger than either alone, from the moment that he folded his arms about her naked body, and felt hers encircle his own, Harold had a sense of having been created anew.

Since the moment of his initiation, fucking had been to Harold one of the great joys of life, perhaps in fact the greatest. He had screwed his way through twelve years of young manhood, spewing forth his sperm in great streams of delight, into the bodies of women, by the front and by the back, into their mouths and between their breasts, sent it arching through the air for the delectation of the curious, and always coming back for more, priding himself on his ability to give women their pleasure even as he took his own. Harold was good at fucking, and he knew it, and he was proud of it. There were times, low times, when he even thought it might be his greatest talent, his one truly golden asset. Well and truly had he fucked through the years, and he would not ever denigrate those hours of pleasure; yet he became convinced in the small confines of Hope's green and yellow bedroom that he had never, in all that time, made love. To make love was most certainly to fuck, but to fuck was not necessarily to make love. He had always known that, at the back of his mind—even his cock had known it in its way—but his cock had striven mightily to deny that it knew it, and his mind had been eager to agree.

Not that it mattered, now that he knew better.

"Do you remember," Hope asked, "how startled I was when you suggested we meet again that afternoon when you came back here from the march?"

"Yes," said Harold. "I thought you must have a boy friend."

She shook her head, smiling up at him. "No. It was just that I simply hadn't realized that there was nothing to stop you from walking out the door and never appearing in my life again. It just hadn't occurred to me at all."

Harold pressed her tightly to him. "Thank God," he said, "that I knew enough to take advantage of my luck."

*   *   *

"I think I've fallen in love," said Harold, who was having trouble getting used to the words although not the idea. "I mean, I know I have."

"Corrupted at last," said Spike, offering his hand. "I knew you could do it if you really put your heart into it."

"It's not something I was trying to do," said Harold. "It just sort of happened that way."

"Naturally," said Spike. "It's not something you can plan. In fact, once it's happened, it has a tendency to plan you."

"So I've noticed," said Harold. "Every time I make a decision I find myself wondering how Hope will react.

"Hope," said Spike. "So that's her name. I assume she's the same girl you met at the peace march, the one you've been acting so coy about for the past three weeks?"

"I haven't been acting coy," said Harold indignantly, stung by the realization that he had been.

"Oh, come off it, Harold. There were all those hints that you were seeing somebody new and interesting, but then after whetting my appetite with some mysterious tidbit or other you'd clam right up again."

"Well," said Harold with a defensive note in his voice, "I didn't want to talk about something I wasn't even sure was happening."

"Sure what was happening, Harold? You're not being very communicative even now. Or is your mind clouded by romance."

"Probably," said Harold, feeling quite pleased at the idea. "But what I meant was that I didn't really think I was falling in love with Hope. I mean, I hardly even had any sexual interest in her at all the first couple of times I saw her. Not that she isn't attractive. She's lovely. But for some reason I wasn't turned on right away. I'll never understand why not."

"Sometimes," said Spike, "I can hardly credit your naïveté, Harold."

"What naïveté?" asked Harold, feeling naïve.

"For one thing, my friend, you seem to be awfully confused about the relationship between love and sex. In fact, that might be one good reason why it took you so fucking long to fall in love with someone."

"All right," said Harold. "Go ahead, tell me about myself. Explain my stupidity to me."

"I'm sure it's not stupidity, Harold," said Spike, with a reassuring pat on the back that only called attention to the purr of condescension in his voice. "You're hardly a stupid person. I suspect it's something more along the lines of a personality disorder."

"You mean I'm warped," said Harold. "You might as well say it right out. I can take it."

"Oh, I think warped is too strong a term," said Spike. "It's just that your attitudes about sex and love seem awfully inflexible. It's perfectly possible, you know, for someone to fall in love with someone without going to bed with them."

"Not in my case," said Harold.

"Are you quite sure?"

"Certainly," said Harold, with some inkling that he was painting himself into a corner.

"Well, if so, which I doubt, you're the exception that proves the rule. There are millions of people, you know, who never slept with their spouses until after the wedding."

"No wonder there are so many divorces," said Harold. "Besides, although it may be possible to fall in love with someone before going to bed with them, it's just as possible to fall in love with them after you've been to bed. You can't deny that."

"I wouldn't think of denying it, Harold. I'm sure that many people who fall in love before going to bed with one another fall even more deeply in love after they've finally had sex. All I'm trying to do is point out to you that your statement about not believing you were falling in love *because* you had no strong sexual interest was specious."

"No, it wasn't," said Harold. "Because I didn't fall in love with Hope until after I'd been to bed with her."

"That's what you think," said Spike.

"And you know better, I suppose?"

"Well, it does occur to me that you must have been falling in love with Hope before you knew you were, or else you wouldn't have been so coy about her existence."

"I don't follow that at all," said Harold with some satisfaction.

"It's just not like you to be coy about the women in your life, Harold, that's all. How much and what kinds of things you say about a woman seem to have a lot to do with whether you respect her or not. The less you respect a woman, the more you're likely to tell about her, including her sexual attributes and proclivities. But if you do respect her, then you talk only about her personality. I've never known you to be actively mysterious about a woman, though, except in the case of Hope. In fact, I was beginning to wonder if you'd turned queer in your old age, you were behaving so oddly."

Harold gave Spike the finger.

"The only other deviation I could think of that might explain your actions was that you were falling in love. And given your advanced age and past history, you'll have to admit that falling in love can only be regarded as deviant behavior."

"I haven't even turned thirty yet," said Harold.

"For falling in love for the first time, Harold, that's old, old, old."

"So you're telling me that I was falling in love with Hope right from the start and didn't even know it?" Harold certainly wasn't going to admit that the same thought had occurred to him.

"Not only that, Harold. I'm telling you that I knew it before you did. I've just been waiting for the announcement."

Harold was appalled. "The arrogance," he muttered. "The incredible gall of some people."

"I imagine Marge has realized, too," said Spike quietly.

"What do you mean?" Harold knew very well what Spike meant, but it was a problem he wanted to pretend didn't exist for as long as possible.

"Have you told her about what's going on?"

"Not yet," said Harold.

"Let me give you some advice, Harold," said Spike. "Tell her before she tells you."

"Jesus Christ," said Harold. "How did I get into this mess, anyway?"

"Don't take it so hard, Harold. It's just a part of growing up."

* * *

"All right," said Marge briskly. "Now that I have a drink in front of me, what's this mysterious subject we have to have a talk about? You were at such pains to get us together in neutral territory, it must be something momentous. Are we going to have our own little Yalta agreement?"

Harold was certainly glad he had a drink in front of him. If Marge possessed any one quality that gave him particular cause for regret, it was her ability to stay one step ahead of him. In spite of his efforts to disguise the fact, she was quite right about his desire to meet on neutral ground. He had been thinking about her as well as himself, however. It was not a scene that he thought should take place in the apartment of either of them. Lunch, he had determined in the course of two days of worrying the problem into the ground, would be the best time for the confrontation, so that the subsequent press of afternoon work might be allowed to exercise its busy balm.

But having decided upon a luncheon meeting, there was still the question of where. It had to be a restaurant where it was possible to talk without screaming, yet not so quiet that conversation was easily overheard from one table to the next. Bad service was a further requirement: Harold felt there were few things more inhibiting to private conversation than the hovering presence of servants or waiters. He had never been able to muster his mother's aristocratic disregard for the humanity of servants. She felt no compunction whatever about discussing private matters in front of them, and had even been known to pass judgment on their very competence when they were out of sight but not earshot in the next room. Yet she could never understand why her servants were always quitting. Harold supposed she must be blissfully happy in Greece with her shipowner—the servants were too numerous to count and understood practically no English at all.

Harold's mind was drifting, as it was inclined to do at moments of stress. He glanced at Marge and, fudging further, asked, "How's your drink?"

"It's a drink," said Marge. "Who could ask for anything more?"

Harold had chosen a very expensive (and thus not overcrowded) French restaurant with really terrible service. The tables, moreover, were placed unusually far apart, in order to provide ample room in which incompetent waiters might negotiate back and forth with the hors d'oeuvre cart, the pastry cart, and (terror on wheels) the flambéed whatsis cart. A year ago, Harold had witnessed a spectacular collision between the hors d'oeuvre cart and the pastry cart, resulting in the creation of such gourmet treats as *Napoléon à la vinaigrette* and artichoke hearts with whipped cream and maraschino cherries.

"What are you grinning at, Harold?"

"Oh, nothing really," said Harold. He waved a hand. "It's too complicated to explain."

"That seems to go for a lot of things, doesn't it? Look, would you like me to tell you what it is you brought me here to tell me?"

Harold was shamed into action. Pulling himself together, he blurted, "I think I've fallen in love," with all the firmness of a seventeen-year-old.

"Of course," said Marge, displaying her Junoesque dignity at its most condescending—with some justification, Harold had to admit. "I really didn't believe you'd been avoiding me because of a cold," Marge continued. "The usual note of self-pity was missing."

Harold hadn't seen Marge since the night before he and

Hope had gone to *The Fox* and to bed. "I'm sorry, Marge," he said. "I just didn't know my own mind. I had to sort things out a bit."

"Fine, Harold. That I can understand. But are you sure you managed to get them sorted out? You seem rather vague."

"Yes, I'm sure." Harold looked into Marge's eyes and managed not to blink.

"Then why do you say you *think* you're in love? Or was that just an exercise in verbal chicken shit?"

Harold felt foolish, and more nervous than ever. If he was going to keep any kind of control over the situation, he was obviously going to have to get a move on. "Chicken shit," he said. "As you so charmingly put it."

"It's serious, then?"

"Yes," said Harold, with an odd hallucinatory feeling that Marge was being transformed into somebody's mother-in-law right in front of his eyes.

"Are you going to marry her?" asked Marge. She moved her shoulders as though she were readjusting a stole, undoubtedly sable.

"I plan to ask her," said Harold.

"Wanted to get me decently buried first, I gather."

Harold said nothing. He felt bleak.

But Marge suddenly smiled. "I'm being a bitch," she said. "Actually, I think that was a very nice and very proper instinct. I'm sure this isn't any easier for you than me, Harold. Maybe even harder."

Harold wasn't sure whether at this juncture he more greatly feared a bitchy Marge or an ultra-rational Marge. "I have been finding things pretty confused," he said.

"What's the girl like?" Marge asked silkily.

Harold did not really know how to describe Hope. His own feelings about her had developed so suddenly, and the things that charmed him most about her were so personal, that he doubted his ability to describe her with sufficient objectivity for anyone else to get a very clear picture of her.

"She's writing her Ph.D. thesis," said Harold, starting with the most clearcut fact in his possession. "On an Italian painter."

"What painter?"

"Solimena. Seventeenth century."

"How obscure," said Marge.

"I thought obscurity was the essence of thesis writing," said Harold, a trifle defensively. "Anyway, I don't think she takes it all too seriously."

"I hope not, for your sake. She a New York girl?"

"No. Boston. Her father's a brain surgeon."

"A brain surgeon from Boston. My, my. Very high class."

Harold's fingers tightened around his glass. This was going to get worse, he was sure. Marge was playing it very cool and above it all, which meant she was trembling on the edge of outright sarcasm. He was sure she would plummet over the edge eventually.

"Well, we've established that she's brainy and wellborn," said Marge. "Is she also beautiful?"

"Not in any flashy way," said Harold. "Men wouldn't turn to look at her in the street."

Since Harold had once told Marge he liked walking down the street with her because so many men turned to get another look at her, he quickly realized he'd made a mistake.

"So that's how you define flashy, is it?" said Marge. "I'm happy to have men look at me, but I'm not at all sure I like being called flashy."

"I didn't mean it that way, Marge."

"No? Well, anyway, men who have flashy wives usually have flashy ex-wives sooner or later. So I guess you're lucky to have found a more demure beauty for yourself."

"I'm not married yet," said Harold, feeling irritated. "She might even refuse."

"She's a fool if she does," Marge snapped.

Harold looked up, sharply. Their eyes met and Marge, who appeared to be slightly flushed, said, "That's a compliment, by the way."

"Thank you," said Harold. "Since it's a compliment."

It was Marge's turn to sigh, which caused Harold momentarily to stop being nervous for himself and to feel sorry for Marge instead.

"Not that I feel I'm a fool, you understand. We would hardly have been the happiest of married couples. As I'm sure you'll agree."

Harold nodded. "But I'm very glad we had what we did." Which was a lame remark, and banal to boot, yet there was nothing else in his head.

Marge looked at him for a moment as though she might say something sharp about his way with the language. But all she did say was, "So am I."

Harold was considerably disconcerted by a sudden small leap of his cock, in salute to past pleasures.

"You haven't told me her name," said Marge, reaching for her glass.

"Her name is Hope," said Harold.

"That figures," said Marge.

*   *   *

Harold proposed to Hope at 1:15 A.M., as they sat naked in Hope's bed sharing a piece of lemon meringue pie off the same plate. "Let's get married," he suggested, in as casual a tone as he could muster.

"You like the domestic life, do you?" Hope asked. She smiled at him and took another bite of pie.

"I'm serious," said Harold, who was afraid he'd sounded a little too casual.

"I know."

Harold felt as vulnerable as a fifteen-year-old inviting a girl to the school prom. "Will you marry me?" he said.

"Yes," said Hope, and smiled still more, looking amused as well as happy.

"We can get the blood tests tomorrow and the license on Friday," said Harold, feeling a great need to get the details settled immediately.

Hope's expression changed. She hesitated for a moment. "I don't want to do it that way, Hal," she said, very seriously.

"What way?" Harold was confused.

"The registry office way."

"Oh," said Harold.

"It wouldn't be fair to my parents," Hope said.

Harold looked down at the plate of unfinished pie between them. He hadn't given much thought to Hope's parents. Certainly, though, the last thing he wanted to do was to involve his own mother and father in the proceedings. Getting married was a big enough step in itself, and he wanted to keep the side effects down to a minimum.

"I just wanted to make things as simple as possible," he said.

"I know. And I guess it's silly, but I'd feel guilty if we did it that way."

"What do you mean, 'feel guilty'? Getting married is something you do for yourself, not your parents." Harold found this reminder of the conventionality of Hope's background something of a jolt. Not that he objected to the conventional side of Hope's own personality—in fact, her stability, her plain old-fashioned niceness, her happy lack of chic neurotic symptoms were among the things that had attracted him to her in the first place. Her parents, though, were quite a different matter. A crazy lady like Marge's mother he knew how to handle: his own upbringing had prepared him admirably for dealing with the crazies. But the thought of coping with a set of more usual in-laws made him feel decidedly insecure.

"Of course one gets married for oneself," said Hope. "But I don't see why my parents should be deprived of the pleasure of giving me a wedding without a good reason. And it's not as though they're going to try to stop me, or anything."

"You're quite sure?" asked Harold, his insecurity blossoming into paranoia. "A free-lance director isn't what every parent would choose for a son-in-law."

"Oh, come on, Hal. Don't be ridiculous."

Harold sighed. "Well, then, there's my mother. Wait till they meet her."

"Wait till you meet my Aunt Martha," Hope said.

Harold looked sour. He was trying not to, but he knew that he did.

"Hal, you're being silly. It's not going to hurt us to do it the usual way. It would make my parents happy, and it would make me feel better." Hope touched his arm. "I really kind of look forward to it, to be honest."

Harold managed to prevent himself from sighing again. "I don't want to spoil anything for you," he said. "How long would we have to wait?"

"Not long. I guess it would take about a month to get everything arranged." Hope gave him a teasing smile. "Are you afraid you'll change your mind?"

"Of course not," said Harold, squeezing her thigh. The thought of delay did disturb him, though. He loved Hope, he was certain. And he wanted to marry her; he was also sure of that. But he wanted to do it right away. He wanted to put his old life behind him and embark on this new one without any pause. In this case, transitions made him nervous. Once it was done, he was sure he would not regret it. But he didn't want to have a lot of time to think about the implications of it all beforehand.

The thought of a big church wedding only increased his apprehension. You never knew who might show up at one of those affairs. Harold had a sudden ghastly image of an irate cadre of former girl friends, led by Marge in a Wonder Woman costume, lining up to throw tomatoes at him as he came out of the church. "Okay," he said, stoically. "It's just that big church weddings always seem to be such a trauma. I guess they're supposed to be. Rites of passage and all that."

"Good God," said Hope, "I don't want a big church wedding. I was thinking of just a simple ceremony in my parents' living room. Thirty people at the most. In fact, if we're going to get Aunt Martha into the room we'd better make it twenty-five."

"Oh, well," said Harold, with a modicum of relief. "That's not so bad. I thought you were talking about all the trimmings." Harold reasoned with himself. Marriage was, so they said, a matter of compromise. He had certainly got thoroughly tired of his uncompromising relationship with Marge. It seemed a good time to start looking at things from a different point of view.

"It won't be so bad," said Hope.

Harold determined to be grown-up about it. "I'm sure it won't," he said.

He smiled at Hope. "I'm sure it won't," he repeated.

10 / Rites

Harold gazed out the second-best bedroom window at the patrician red brick of Beacon Hill houses and the lustrous green leaves of Beacon Hill trees. The brick looked old yet unworn, the leaves might have been personally colored by Monet. A calm, secure, lulling scene, without doubt, but it was having no such effect on Harold. In thrall to behavioral clichés, Harold was nervous as any groom.

You could argue, he supposed, that the confusion of emotions he felt was only natural, a reassuring sign of his ultimate humanity. But Harold was not disposed to go easy on himself. By his twenty-ninth year, it seemed to him, he really ought to have been able to exorcise from his system the fevers of adolescence, those alternating chills (of abject uncertainty) and hot flashes (of rabid sexuality) that he had once believed would pass from him instantaneously upon the loss of his cherry, but which had persisted through the years in one guise or another, afflicting sometimes his body and sometimes his brain, striking always without warning yet with ludicrous effect.

Here he was on his wedding day, sundered by the banal traumas of a Norman Rockwell groom, his palms sweaty and his eyes dark-rimmed. Suddenly, he would be possessed by wild racing fears of marital captivity, clipped wings and gilded cages for the once proud hawk. Such fears were plainly idiotic, for he had long since begun to see that the supposed freedom of his bachelorhood was a cage of another sort, a tawdry chicken-wire affair from which he fervently wished to escape—just how fervently he had admitted to himself only since Hope had said, "Yes."

Harold experienced a hot flash, chasing the fearful chills and infecting him instead with abruptly leaping anticipations of sexual intimacy—in spite of the fact that he'd been sleeping with Hope since the middle of May. He had not slept with her last night, however, here in her own house, an exercise in self-deprivation that would never again, thank God, have to be repeated. It had been a ghastly night. He had had insomnia, felt insatiably sexy, and fought a victorious but exhausting (and ultimately Pyrrhic) battle to keep his hands off his frothing private parts, which, when he finally drifted off to fretful sleep, took immediate revenge upon him by producing an unaided ejaculation, one that limned Mrs. Richardson's impeccable percales with stains positively orgiastic in scope.

Harold went across the room to the straight-backed chair where his suit coat was hanging; otherwise he had been dressed for almost forty minutes. And the wedding guests weren't due for nearly an hour. Only Spike, who was to be his best man, and a girl named Susan Kelly, Hope's matron of honor, would be here sooner. Harold looked at his suitcase, repacked and ready to go. In it, under the resort clothes he would be wearing for the next ten days, was a script in a black binder. In spite of the fact that it might prove to be the basis for his first feature film, if all the pieces, financial and otherwise, fell into place, he had been unable to give his mind over to it for the past several days. He wished that he were the kind of man who could, at this very moment, take it out and sit down to ponder, once again, its possibilities. But he wasn't that kind of man, and so he turned away and went out of his room.

He proceeded quietly down the hall, past the best bedroom, a territory occupied by Hope's Great Aunt Martha, who was certainly great in girth and whose face gave startling intimations of past family scandal in the form of sexual congress with a Boston Bull. Hope's mother had apologized to Harold for putting him in the smaller room on the street side, but explained that Aunt Martha was accustomed to staying in the other room whenever she visited, and that it was unwise to attempt to teach her new tricks since her bite was as bad as her bark.

At the bottom of the stairs, Harold turned toward the back of the house, intending to take a stroll around the walled garden that Aunt Martha's room overlooked (the view of this cloistered square of shrubbery and flower beds being the prime element in making the best guestroom best). A scent of roses filtered into the house through the screen door at the back of the downstairs hallway, and as Harold caught the rich, sweet smell, he quickened his steps over the polished floor and oriental scatter rugs. Before he reached the door, however, the voice of Hope's father accosted him from the study, which lay directly beneath Aunt Martha's room and commanded its own privileged view of the sunlight and shadow among the roses.

"Hello, Harold." Dr. Richardson's voice was a smooth, measured, rather somber baritone.

"Oh, hello, sir."

Dr. Richardson made Harold feel like a student again; when they first met, Harold had known instantly, out of retrograde instinct, that the doctor should be addressed as "sir." No more intimate term had since been suggested, and Harold suspected that this respectful form of address was one of the few things the doctor approved of in his prospective son-in-law. A free-lance film director and former college dropout with divorced parents—it was hardly, Harold thought again, what the man would have chosen for his Hope.

The doctor leaned back in the elegant Chippendale chair before his immaculate mahogany desk. "Feeling restless, are you," he said. It was a statement, not a question.

"I'd just as soon have it over with," said Harold, and was unable to control the surly undertone to his voice. "But I guess that's what the groom usually feels," he added more lightly, using as a shield exactly those emotions he had been busy despising in himself a few minutes earlier.

"I suppose," said Dr. Richardson. "Although I daresay that in some cases the anticipation and suspense are greater than in others." These words were pronounced with such consummate dryness that Harold found it difficult to decide whether they were intended as a rebuke or as an acknowledgment of complicity. Hope had told him that before their marriage, her parents had lived together secretly for almost eighteen months, but even so Harold had the impression the doctor disapproved, however irrationally, of similar behavior in his daughter. Or perhaps, since he so obviously prided himself on his rationality, his disapproval was reserved for his daughter's choice of partner rather than being aroused by the act itself.

Harold looked around the study, which was overflowing with the brilliant light of a July noon. It was a beautiful room, square and high-ceilinged, with two large windows on the book-lined west wall and a double set of French windows leading into the garden. Opposite the French windows was a stone fireplace, painted black, its mantle surmounted by a handsome portrait of the doctor's grandfather, whose rather cold blue eyes the doctor, but not Hope, had inherited. The fourth wall was hung with a collection of old-master drawings, mostly Flemish and German, on medical subjects. Harold supposed, rather reluctantly, that Hope's interest in art must derive from her father.

"I like this house very much," Harold said, and was sincere.

"I'm very glad," said the doctor. "It may, after all, one day be yours. If you manage to stay married long enough."

Harold smiled, oddly unshocked. He found this frontal attack less disturbing and easier to cope with than the distant irony the doctor usually employed. "You don't really trust me, sir, do you?" Harold said in an offhand, conversational tone.

"Ah, well," said the doctor, pointing his chin like William F. Buckley. "I doubt that any man with an only daughter quite trusts his prospective son-in-law."

"I must say I'm curious," Harold said in a slightly harder voice, "as to which of my many liabilities you find most disturbing."

For an instant the doctor looked startled. There was perhaps some slight thawing of the icy surface of his eyes. "Don't misunderstand me, Harold. I can quite see that many parents would regard you as a very good catch. And I can also see that my daughter is very much in love with you. My only concern is for the, shall we say, milieu in which you live and work. The entertainment world has never struck me as being particularly conducive to a stable marriage. Long separations seem to be so common, and sexual partners so available."

"I wouldn't have thought that you were the sort to subscribe to *Screen World*, doctor," said Harold, surprising himself with the degree of anger in his voice. "Fortunately, Hope doesn't have a theatrical career of her own, so there's nothing to prevent her from accompanying me wherever it's necessary for me to go."

"And if there are children? Or aren't you planning on children?"

"Eventually," said Harold. "But not for some time." Harold was still adjusting, in fact, to the idea of having children, a thought that had always seemed rather frightening in the abstract, but which was coming to seem surprisingly attractive when specifically associated with Hope. Harold was even emboldened, by his new sense of life's possibilities, to suspect that he might be a good father. At least he would be a better one than his own had been—of that he was certain. "Even when there are children," he continued, "and it becomes necessary for me to stay away for some time, I don't really see that it's anything to worry about. Separation can sometimes be good for people. I know at least two men who are playing around exactly because they're so bored with seeing their wives all the time. That's a negative argument, I realize, but just to be obnoxious, I'll throw in another one. Secretaries are even easier to lay than starlets."

Dr. Richardson's long, subtle hands lay quietly before him on his shining desk. "I'm glad that I made you angry, Harold," he said. "I would have been disappointed if I'd failed to."

It was the moment, Harold knew, for them both to laugh and shake hands. "Call me Sandy," Dr. Alexander Richardson would say, and they would become fast friends. But Harold was still angry—he did not quite know why. He couldn't even smile. It took all his effort to speak calmly. "I'm sorry you felt it was necessary to provoke me," he said.

Dr. Richardson, in reply, did not ask Harold to call him Sandy. He said, merely, "It will take a while, I imagine, for us to know one another."

Harold, recalling how he had loathed Sam Lazer when he had first known him, could only hope that further acquaintance with Dr. Richardson would bring a similar appreciation of hidden virtues. It was very strange, really; Harold was convinced that he would have immediately accepted Dr. Richardson as a stepfather, back when he was seventeen, and would have just as immediately taken delight in Sam Lazer as a father-in-law now that he was about to turn thirty. But each man, unhappily, had been cast in the opposite role.

*   *   *

"You look as though you were going to a funeral instead of your own wedding," Spike said.

"Wait until it's your turn next month," Harold said grimly.

They had been left to their own devices while Dr. Richardson went into the garden to have a last look at the efforts of the caterer. They were to be served lobster newburg, Harold had discovered without surprise.

Spike sighed. "I wish to hell I was getting married today. The planning for our great event is beginning to resemble the logistics for a medieval siege."

"That's what you get for allowing yourself to be talked into a big church wedding," said Harold, who didn't really feel like making with the banter. Perhaps it was only his present mood, but Harold suspected that the adolescent excesses of repartee in which he and Spike had indulged with so much pleasure for so many years were beginning to pall. It wasn't that he was less fond of Spike, and he hoped it wasn't that his mind was less quick or his wit less sharp, but the events of his life did not seem to lend themselves as well to frivolity as they once had. He and Spike had been playing a farce for years. It was no longer appropriate to their lives, but Harold thought it would take a while to make the transition to a more subtle, if less brilliant, form of dialogue.

"How did you manage to avoid a big wedding?" Spike asked. He was mixing himself a drink from the doctor's private bar, whose contents had been urged upon them.

"Hope just told her parents she was going to be married at home and by a judge or else she'd do it in a registry office without prior announcement."

"Barbara said that if we didn't have a church wedding we'd be disinherited," Spike said glumly, and sipped his drink.

"I didn't know Presbyterians were so religious," said Harold.

"It's a matter of social standing, you idiot, not religious fervor. So far as I can tell, Barbara's parents think of God as that big caterer in the sky."

"Oh, well," said Harold. "From that point of view, I'm sure the Richardsons, or the good doctor at least, are delighted not to have to expose me to any more of their circle than absolutely necessary."

"Come off it, Harold. Mrs. Richardson not only thinks you're charming but the best-looking male Hope has ever shown any interest in."

Harold did not even made an effort not to be pleased. He was in need of flattery. "She's charming herself," he said. "And Hope obviously inherited her personality. The doctor, however, is convinced we're headed for an early divorce."

"What?"

"Ah, well, you see, it's the lascivious and amoral nature of the entertainment world, as he calls it. Besides that, he has me pegged as the original two-timer. Or perhaps I should say philanderer." Harold still felt angry; but now he thought perhaps he was beginning to understand why.

"What crap," said Spike. "I hope you told the old bastard off." He looked over his shoulder at the door of the room and took a nervous gulp from his glass.

Harold smiled. "One's courage is not what it might be in the doctor's presence. I did make some smart-aleck remark, though, no doubt only convincing him further of my lack of respect for conventional wisdom. Anyway, he's right."

"What do you mean he's right?"

"Well, that happens to be something that worries me, to be honest."

"What does, for Christ's sake?"

"The lascivious and amoral nature of the entertainment world."

"Look, Harold, I'm going to pour you a drink and you're going to drink it. So you might as well state a preference."

"Scotch," said Harold. "But I'm perfectly serious."

"I know you're serious. That's why I insist you take a drink. It might clear your crazy head."

"I love Hope," Harold said quietly. "But I've never been faithful to anyone in my life. I mean I've never even tried. It wasn't expected with Marge, on either side, and there hasn't been anyone else who mattered enough."

"Exactly," said Spike. "Since Hope matters enough for you to marry her, she'll matter enough for you to be faithful to her. I really wouldn't worry about it, Harold."

Harold gave a tight, sardonic smile and accepted his drink. "Actually," he said, "I would have thought that worrying about it was a good sign. I mean it proves that I care."

"All right, Harold. If it makes you feel any better, then worry about it. Whatever you say. I agree with you in advance."

"You're much too agreeable to be any help at all," said Harold. "I suppose you don't worry in the least about being faithful to Barbara."

"No, Harold, I don't. But then, I never was a self-proclaimed sex maniac."

"I wasn't asking you to get actively unpleasant," said Harold.

"Look, Harold, take it from me, you're a wonderful guy and you're marrying a lovely girl and you're going to be sickeningly happy. Now shut up and enjoy it."

"If you say so," said Harold, and managed a grin. He took a big swig of his scotch.

"And now that you've got some of that stuff inside you, I also have a letter for you from your ex-mistress."

"Oh, Christ," said Harold, taking another swig of scotch.

"Marge promised me it had only nice things to say," said Spike. "And I promised her I'd make you read it."

"Give it to me," said Harold. "I'll read it later."

"That would be in bad taste, Harold. You don't read letters from ex-mistresses while your new wife is in the powder room on the plane to the Bahamas. It just isn't done."

"All right, all right," said Harold. "I'll read it now." He felt reluctant, but didn't know why. He believed Spike that

Marge would have only nice things to say. Perhaps he was afraid that it would make him miss her, which was not something he wanted to do at all.

*　　*　　*

Dear Harold,

I wanted to be able to wish you well on your wedding day and this seemed the best way to do it; it's so easy to get into trouble on the telephone and the last thing I want is to cause any bad feeling. I'm very glad that you're getting married. It's the right thing for you to do and the right time for you to do it. Everything was rapidly coming unstuck between you and me, and there were only two possible ways you could have gone once the glue evaporated altogether: either you would have got married or you would have gone back to screwing a girl a night. You've had enough of the latter diversion over the years, to judge by what you've told me and I'm sure you've told me only a part of it. Of course, after a few more years of screwing around you might have got married anyway, but you would've wasted the best years for marriage. You're the right age now, just right, and on top of that you're starting to be really successful. That first great success, they always say, is sweetest if you've got someone to share it with. Besides, you're the kind of man who ought to be married. I know you used not to think so, but that was because you were always working so hard to keep the vulnerable parts of you hidden away where no one could get at them. So long as they weren't on display, no one could even be said to ignore them, the way your parents chose to. (Excuse the amateur psychiatry; I'd take it out but this is the third time I've typed this thing over, and I promised myself I'd keep going.) Anyway, Hal (which I never managed to get in the habit of calling you), I think you'll discover more and more about the pleasures that can come from opening yourself up, and I think you can do it without losing any of the qualities that make you interesting already. Your Hope, in other words, is a lucky girl.

I suppose it seems odd that I should be saying these things, since the likelihood of my getting married is very small indeed. I can't imagine getting married for any other reason than money, and with Poppy failing so fast, I'll soon have more than enough of that to fulfill my admittedly expensive but nevertheless sensible tastes. Unlike your crazy mother, I am not turned on by swarthy Greeks or 150-foot yachts, and I think gambling casinos are the dullest places in creation. But the main thing is that I don't have your hidden need of familial warmth. And it's just because I don't have it that I was able to see it in you so clearly. In a way I'm sorry I wasn't able to answer that need, but at least we had some very good fun together—and I even think that by not being what you needed I helped you recognize that you wanted something different from what you'd always told yourself you did.

I hope you'll feel that it's possible for us to keep in touch. I don't expect Hope would want to have me over to the house every other Tuesday, but it would be nice if you and I could have lunch once in a while. If you don't feel easy about that at first—or even never do—well, I will understand. It would make me sad, but I'd understand.

Anyway, Harold, Hal that is, please know that I want you to have the very happiest of marriages and the most successful of careers. I'm not sending a wedding present, it seems like lousy taste somehow. And I hope you won't think I'm an arrogant bitch if I say that in some small way I feel that my wedding present to you is yourself.

As ever,
Marge

*   *   *

The Judge was a distinguished-looking man with hair of a silvery whiteness perfectly suited to his role. His hands, which he held clasped in front of him, were exquisitely man-

icured. From his position in front of the fireplace, he gazed
with rapt benignity at the twenty-odd guests standing and
sitting around the perimeter of the large square living room,
his face suffused by one of those permanent but essentially
unfocused and non-commital smiles Harold associated with
politicians and clergymen. Since he was on this afternoon
substituting for the usual clergyman, and might once have
been a politician, the Judge's smile was, of course, entirely
appropriate. On further reflection, however, Harold doubted
that Dr. Richardson would have as a family friend any man
vulgar enough to present himself as a political candidate,
unless perhaps it had been in the role of sacrificial lamb in a
hopeless cause. In fact, the only note of vulgarity Harold
could detect in the entire group gathered in the living room
was struck by Aunt Martha, who had swathed herself in
yards of mauve velvet despite the July heat. His own mother's gold sandals (she had been evidencing a more Mediterranean taste lately) might constitute one other note of vulgarity, but they could hardly be considered Dr. Richardson's
responsibility.

Harold, standing at the Judge's left with Spike behind
him, glanced back at his mother once again. Noticing, she
bestowed upon him her gayest smile. She was clearly very
happy these days, traipsing about the world with her Greek,
and even though she had not married him she appeared to
be more secure than in the past—or perhaps she was just
more fatalistic. Harold was convinced that it was his mother
and not the Greek who was resisting marriage; she had said
something in a letter about Greek men being positively
archetypal in their tendency to treat their mistresses better
than their wives, and it seemed entirely possible that she
found the role of mistress both more congenial and more
reassuring. "To lose a lover," she had said once, "is sometimes sadder but certainly far less damaging to one's pride
than to lose a husband."

One of the two husbands she had lost stood next to her on

this day. Harold was astonished at how cordial his father and mother had been to one another—far more friendly than appearance's sake might ordain. Harold could not help wondering, too, whether or not it seemed strange to his father to be attending the wedding of one son, in the at least temporary company of the woman who had given birth to that child, while another son who had only just begun to walk remained at home with the woman who had given birth to him. Surely, it seemed to Harold, there must be at least some sense of dislocation. On the other hand, given his father, perhaps not.

As he stood waiting for Hope to enter the room, looking across at his parents, it suddenly occurred to Harold that he had never attended a wedding at which some member of either the bride or the groom's immediate family had not been through a divorce. Marge's letter had restored Harold's calm and his good spirits, but this new thought shocked him into a renewed nervousness. Only the other day he had read in the paper that in California more people were getting divorced than were getting married. Of course, Harold and Hope were getting married in Massachusetts, where the statistics were undoubtably more favorable to marriage, it being such a Catholic state; on the other hand, it was entirely likely that they would move to California eventually.

Harold's palms began to hurt. His fingers were so tightly clenched that the nails were cutting into the flesh. Would Hope be able to see it, he wondered, as a sign of his true love for her and desire not to hurt her, if he were to vault Aunt Martha's massive mauveness and disappear out the open French windows behind her?

This image caused Harold to grin, to take pleasure once again in his own absurdity; he had been aware of that absurdity all day, but until now it had given him no pleasure. And as he grinned, at the exact moment, it seemed to Harold, Hope appeared in the doorway of the living room, her arm resting lightly on her father's. Her light brown hair loosely framed the long oval of her face, which was lightly tanned from afternoons spent with Harold on a plaid blanket in Central Park. She wore a pale green suit of raw silk and, as she entered the room, she turned her green eyes toward Harold and saw his grin. Their eyes met.

Harold could see nothing else. Except for Hope's eyes, the room might just as well have been empty. As she advanced across the empty space between them, Hope smiled at Harold, as if in answer to the grin that had suddenly appeared upon and continued to be spread across his face.

ABOUT THE AUTHOR

John Malone grew up on the campus of Phillips Academy, Andover, where his father taught American history. After graduating from Andover, he attended Harvard for three years, dropping out in 1961. He spent the next four years in Europe, first on the island of Ibiza, and subsequently in Rome and London, supporting himself through his writing, various research and editorial projects, and occasional film dubbing. In 1965 he returned to America, taking up residence in New York City, where he has worked ever since as a free-lance editor and ghost writer. Under his own name he has written documentary film scripts, a children's book and numerous short stories, the latter appearing in such publications as *Evergreen Review, Swank, New American Review, Transatlantic Review* and *The Iowa Review*. His story, "The Fugitives," was chosen for *Prize Stories 1973: The O. Henry Awards*. He is presently at work on a new novel.